AF409827

Fangs To

My Blood

Fangs To My Blood

Virginie T.

Translated by Mustapha Naceur

6

« Death begets death »

In the remote lands of Russia, life is already difficult of origin, in the Middle Ages. However, life in the service of Lord Vladimir is a real hell. He does not realize all the privileges granted to him by the tsar. He has wealth, women and food in abundance without even lifting a hand, while his people die of hunger and cold working in the fields, but nothing is ever enough. It's really an impossible mission to serve someone who is never satisfied like Vladimir. He always wants more and more, and it is up to me to make sure that his wishes are totally fulfilled. Unfortunately, this time is no exception, he is never satisfied at all.

— Once again! I am disappointed again, Zoran. Do I have to ask you each time to do your job properly?

The Lord's voice raises high so that my humiliation is complete. Whenever he intends to mistreat a servant, he invites his vassals into the great hall. He likes to make public stoning examples to establish his power in this isolated country. He does not need it because no one dares contradict his authority or even think to do so. However, I suspect he enjoys these debasements he does in public.

— The people are poor, my lord…

— Enough pathetic excuses. If they can't afford money to pay the tithe, they only have to send me their daughters as compensation.

His obscene smile scares me. These poor women... their pleading eyes haunt my nights.

— My Lord, they have already sent you all the young girls who are old enough to please you, there are only little girls left…

— Little girls can work until they're old enough to suit me. You make no effort, Zoran, and the other servants begin to think that they will risk nothing to disobey and provoke me.

My fellow wretches can never think that way. I always see them walking along the walls of the castle, with their heads down, silently praying not to be the next to suffer Vladimir's wrath. As I understand them. I wish I were in a less uncomfortable place myself.

When it comes to punishment, my lord has a great sense of imagination. He has a deep affection for ear amputation or tongue piercing. Beheading and the pyre are also his favors. So many torments suffered by servants who have only the misfortune of having found themselves in his path. For these same absurd reasons, I have already lost an ear and my tongue still feels the warmth of the poker that pierced it. I begin to tremble, worrying about the devilish smile displayed by Lord Vladimir. What part of my body is going to have to suffer his wrath? How much more pain am I going to have to endure without flinching and reacting?

— I'm tired of your mistreatment and your flippant attitude.

I see from the corner of my eye Vladimir's most faithful vassals approaching me, encircling me and thus cutting me off any possibility of retreat and escape. My tremors are intensifying. I know for a good reason that amputation will not be appropriate this time. Cutting off my second ear would be of no interest and cutting off one of the four main limbs would prevent me from performing my tasks. Vladimir followed the same stream of thought.

— Mutilate you won't make you any more effective. So, I'm going to make you a visible example to everyone in the country.

My stomach starts clenching. I am afraid of what's

going to happen. Yet, I could not have imagined my punishment, even in my worst nightmares.

— Zoran, by the power I have over you, I sentence you to death. You will be led outside the ramparts at nightfall, then tied up by the four limbs, upside down, and left there until death ensues. What remains of your body will then be thrown into the dung pit, where you belong, if there is anything left after the feast, of course.

I pray that the ball that clogs my throat will kill me before the sentence is carried out. I would not do him with the pleasure of begging him to save me. Too many servants tried and their deaths were even more horrific. Vladimir was increasing their sentence with each plea. Although in my case, I don't see how it could be worse. I'm already on death row. Being driven outside the enclosure means being thrown into the pasture of hungry wolves lurking at night, in search of fresh flesh to devour in these times of winter devastation where no prey remains.

My death was even more painful than my mind could have imagined. The vassals of Vladimir took a malicious pleasure in slashing my body in multiple places so that the smell of blood would attract the wolf packs in a herd. My anxiety became disproportionate as the grunts grew closer. Then the jaws began to snap into the void, each canine wanting to plant its fangs first in my body and fighting between them to have the biggest piece of my person. I prayed that the wolves would fight amongst each other and forget about me. I obviously did not have that chance. The first bite was a real heartbreak for my soul. After all the sacrifices and bad deeds done on behalf of Lord Vladimir, this is how he thanked me. Wolves tore my skin and flesh, feasting on me until I succumbed, to the end. I knew that my soul would go directly to hell after being in the service of Vladimir. One cannot work for a devil man like him as long as keeping his soul. I did not expect to wake up in the dung pit. In fact, I didn't even expect to wake up, at all. Ultimately, death is just the beginning of another life. A life where the prey will become the executioner. Never again will I let a person think they are superior to me. From now on, I would be the sole master of my destiny and the world would tremble before me.

Nowadays

<u>Chapter 1</u>

Tatjana

As far back as I can remember, Koudykina Gora has always seemed grim to me, but it is taking on uncontrollable proportions. Obviously, we are in the middle of winter when the polar cold reigns over the city and this could have had something to do with it. But the problem is not the temperature. Throughout more than two centuries of existence, I have never seen the city so deserted. From the top of my observatory, I see that there are no longer souls living for miles around and boredom threatens to make me fall into a catatonic state. Only mine walk the cobblestone streets, probably looking for their lunch, but there is nothing and nobody to hunt in these places. This doesn't bother me. I don't really have the same diet as my people which is a secret that I treasure very carefully. My father already locks me in my room far too often. Learning my peculiarity will certainly not improve our relationships and will probably not be my ticket out for the outside. A deep sigh breaks my lips when I think of my father. He is not really my father, not in the strict sense of the term as humans understand it. But, undoubtedly, he is my father. Vampires have no children, they have descendants. Finally, they did. I was the last to be created. The last vampire born, the last transformed by the original vampire in person: Zoran. As far as I know, I'm also the only female vampire. Zoran had, until me, only converted men. When I asked him about the reason behind this choice, he replied tactlessly that women are too fickle and that such power should not be in everyone's hands. I personally believe that he refuses to have to share his power with a woman and that he therefore did not want to transform them at the risk of succumbing to the charms of one of them. Today, the question no longer arises since no transformation is allowed anymore by Zoran and he fiercely ensures that this measure is totally respected. Any vampire who has the misfortune to go against this law is inflicted a second death, a death from which he does not rise again. And yes. Summum of supreme power, I am immortal. Pfff, what a joke. It is just a wind to tell the poor so as to scare them. As if they needed more reason to fear us. My people have been so lacking in restraint and discernment that all the surrounding villages have become ghost villages.

Just as empty as the city that sprawls at my feet. There is no longer a human who lives less than fifteen kilometers away and only a few fools in search of the great thrill dare to venture into these woods. Rumors are widespread about the monsters that roam there after dark. No human ever comes out alive, their disappearance fueling rumors a little more. I hear the screams of agony of these unfortunates from my room and it deeply hurts my heart. A heart not entirely dead, by an oddity of chance that Zoran refuses to explain to me. Anyway, He never explains anything to me. I am only a woman, the daughter of a man born at a time when the feminine sex was seen only to give birth. This is something that it is impossible for me to do. It's the irony of fate. It's better that way. I will never impose a life like mine on anyone, not even my worst enemy. I have no use, no future prospects. Zoran is content to hide me from the world. I feel the heavy weight of all the years of loneliness at every moment. Very simply I am frozen in time, out of the world.

— Good morning princess. Slept well?

Anton is my guard. In fact, he is my only connection to the outside world. He is, by force of circumstance, my friend. I needed an ally and he tacitly agreed to be mine. I don't know why. I know he's loyal to my person than to that of our king. And it could cause his final death. In spite of everything, he remains there, by my side. He accedes to all my requests, even the most farfetched, without asking me the slightest question. His daily visit is my only distraction of the day.

— I slept like a dead woman, Anton. Just like every day.

— Hey! I don't see any dead here. We already talked about it, princess. You walk, you talk, so you live.

Although, the fact that Anton is a vampire, he remains a good man, as he should have been during his lifetime. He tries by all means to make me understand that I am more than what I seem to be at first sight. My friend hasn't changed since his transformation, like all of us. His athletic physique makes him a perfect killing machine and his face is always marked with a smile in my company. It's too bad that his faint skin makes him look so… dead. I feel a little angry with him for the condition though I know he is doing it for me. But I can't help it. I can't stand the idea that he would come to see me right after killing someone, even indirectly. So, he never eats before he visits me, which makes him look so white and waxy. He'll take back the colors as soon as he drinks the blood of his next victim that I'd rather not think about.

— Are you hungry, Tatjana?

My stomach rumbles before I can respond, giving him a smile.

— I'll take that as a yes.

— I'm starving.

A tray appears in front of me in a second; a glass filled with red syrupy liquid.

— What do we have here today, Anton? Was the hunt successful?

— Pretty much. Werewolves have been making themselves scarce lately, so the forest is teeming with little beasts. Tonight, I was flushed out of the rabbit hole.

Perfect. I love that. I grab the glass and voraciously drink the blood of this prey which allows me to do without exterminating innocent people. The blood of animals is not as rich as that of human beings, but my satisfaction at not being responsible for the death of someone is more than this sacrifice. Anyway, I don't need to be full of energy to walk around my room over and over again until dawn, a sign that it's a bedtime.

— Your cheeks are rosy. You needed it. You were almost fainter than me.

He's right, the thirst was starting to twist my stomach. I nodded and smiled at him, thanking him.

— Zoran wants to see you.

I lean my head to the side as my smile vanishes. The king rarely calls me near him. I'm his little secret and he keeps me jealously out of sight. As he refuses to show me to my people. My exits require to empty the castle, which does not fail to awake the interest of some curious at each time.

— Do you know why?

— I have no idea, but he wants me to go with you. His summons concerns both of us. The castle has been in ebullience for a few days. Something is coming, but nobody knows what. Besides, Zoran gives orders to everyone without any explanation as well as without any connection between their tasks. He has also sent out of his land all the little unstable vampires.

— I don't understand.

— Me neither, princess. Only Zoran is sufficiently tense. It is wiser to obey and join him without delay in order not to thwart him even more than he is. Prepare yourself. I'll make sure the path is clear.

I nod and keep staring at his place in the room long after he left. I have a strange feeling. The feeling that my whole life will be turned upside down and that I will have a key role in the events to come. Again, one of my little specificities.

I shake myself out of this semi-consciousness and rush to change. My father is struggling to live in our time. He's not trying either, mind you. He was stranded six centuries earlier, at the time of his death, and can't stand to see me in jeans, t-shirts and sneakers like the humans of today. It's really so astonishing compared to the Middle Ages when he was born. I love it. I was able to adapt and evolve thanks to the magazines that my friend regularly brings me from the city. Anton often says that this century sticks more to my personality. He is not wrong. It seems that nowadays, humans think about ecology, recycling and well-being. Yes, I am a bit like that except vegetarianism, since this is a matter of survival for me. You have to believe that I was two centuries ahead of them and that they finally caught up with me. Or that I lived more than I would have expected. In any case, I hurry up to put on a dress that drags on the ground and that suits more to someone of my condition. Notice: the princess of the most powerful king this land has ever seen, the Vampire King Zoran. It's too bad that nobody knows about my existence. This title would have more meaning among people. However, it is just an empty pompous title in my case.

— Are you ready?

The fanatic outburst of Anton makes me jump and my red is now spreading on my cheek instead of my lips.

— Sorry. But Zoran's not tense anymore, he's nervous. We have to go now.

I barely take the time to clean up my mess before I make a scarlet mouth. This red blood makes my skin look even whiter, but Zoran likes to see me wear it.

The corridors are deserted, giving the place a sinister aura; to the point that there is not even a murmur that reaches us. It seems as if the castle had been emptied of all the inhabitants. We reach the king's quarters, recognizable among all by their sumptuous decoration and above all by the poor humans chained to the wall. This vision lifts my stomach. Men and women are held captive without any hope of escape, destined to serve meals to the king and his subjects before being devoured by much worse. These poor bastards are considered only food and not entitled to more account than livestock. The contrast between these filthy and defenseless prey and the gold-embroidered tapestries adorning the walls is really absurd and grotesque. I look away before returning my meal and bow down to my father, who sits in the middle of the room. Protocol, over and over again. Reverence is in order in this realm, for me as well as for other vampires.

— Tatjana. You made yourself desired.

I keep my head down as a sign of repentance.

— Sorry, father. I took the time to put on an outfit that would satisfy you.

It rises with disconcerting ease for a man of six centuries. His steps make no noise on the stone floor, as if he were floating above without touching it. I have no discretion. Too bad, it would allow me to escape from my mausoleum on occasion. He turns around me and I have the unpleasant feeling of being a prey among the raptors.

— You chose well. This white dress suits you perfectly and I love your scarlet lips.

He returns to his seat after a last approving look.

— Stand up. We need to talk.

I execute and scrutinize the face of my father, in search of the slightest clue. His austere gaze reveals nothing of their depth as black as ink. Yet another difference between us. My eyes are bright and Anton confirmed that I was the only vampire in this case.

— This is a serious time. my daughter

— What is going on?

— Come and have a seat here next to me.

Sitting next to him is a very strong word. In reality, I must take my place on my knees, right on the ground before the feet of our leader as a sign of submission, showing the good girl that I am. I realize that I get bitter with time. I feel tired of stagnating in the same place, reduced to having contact only with Zoran and Anton. I dream of integrating into the world and living among the common people. I realize a little bit late the heavy silence that reigns around me. My dad takes off the hood that disguises marks of his old age. It's not a good sign when he takes it off. He only does it when he wants to scare his interlocutor. The people who usually face him think he's funny, but I doubt it. Anton told me how the king intimidates his subjects. Zoran's cruelty is legendary, but seeing the physical stigmata that led him to the throne is another whole story. The absence of one of his ears, as well as his bald scalp marked with countless bites, is a reminder of what he went through before rising from the dead to avenge these executioners. This denotes the strength of his spirit that conquered death itself. He is the very first vampire and creator of our race. The father of all of us.

— Do I bother you, Tatjana ?

His voice is dry, as sharp as a razor blade. I am the princess. However, I am not immune to his anger and the consequences of it. He has already struck me and whipped me for my disobedience. And when it wasn't enough to establish his authority, he went after Anton and attacked him. He knows that despite my condition as a vampire, I have kept my soul and my conscience and that it hurts me much more to watch someone being punished in my place than to be beaten myself. It is my point of weakness and he exploits it deliberately. It is also the threat that he makes me hover if I want to escape. He warned me that he would set the country on fire and blood to find me and that no death would be too much to get me back.

— Absolutely not, my king. I am all ears. You have my full attention.

He takes an extra minute to observe me, as if to probe me and guess what's running through my head, before he starts again.

— Many of our people have disappeared without a trace in recent weeks. They left with their dogs and never came back.

I squeeze my lips not to say that they are not dogs. I've done it before. Once. It cost me a day's lash and three days without eating. I thought I was dying. And when Zoran brought me a human to lift my punishment, I killed that creature without any restraint, tasting his blood on my tongue with unspeakable pleasure until he was bloodless. It was for my survival. The remorse I felt then almost ended me. It was the only time I ever drank human blood and there is no way that it would ever happen again. I'd rather starve than repeat the experience.

— I don't see how I can help you, father. I never leave the castle. So, I don't know where our brothers went or what happened to them.

His voice gets louder and severe.

— Never forget. They are not our brothers. They no more than our subjects; and I know exactly where they are.

Of course. Always this need to be above others. This constant desire for distinction will lead to his loss.

— They are all dead. All of them.

Here we are. When I said that we were not immortal. We are not aging, but we can absolutely die. Again. We become vampires when one of them bites us and leaves us at the gates of death. A dead man does not age anymore. We're living dead, not quite alive and not quite dead. We're stuck in the middle. However, they can end us by burning us alive by the fire or the sun, beheading us or starving. Simply, we are very nice deaths. Although we have an extraordinary capacity for regeneration, we surely can be more or less seriously injured. Well, for the other vampires anyway.

— How do you know if they disappeared?

— I felt the death of those I created. Don't ask stupid questions, will you? This is a serious situation.

Vampire venom is powerful and effectively creates a certain connection between the creator and the creatures. Zoran feels the presence of all the vampires he has begotten. Whereas, we cannot know where Zoran is at all.

— How did they die ? Were they surprised by the sun's rays ?

— Don't talk nonsense. It's only the novices who burn out because of the UV and there haven't been any young vampires for decades. You are the youngest in our nation and you know it.

He takes a break. My father likes to make the suspense last longer.

— Their dogs ripped their throats like the scavengers.

Really, I'm still speechless. I have never seen one, and I can hear the sounds of broken bones during their evening meal. But I can't imagine such a thing. Why ? Why would they do that? They've lived with us as long as I can remember.

Chapter 2

Adrian

I didn't think I could get away so early in the evening, but Anton asked me to go for a walk for a few hours and come back just before dawn. That sounds good. I'll take opportunity to join mine and listen to Dumitru's latest recommendations. Our leader has decided to launch the assault soon. We have to be ready. The pack is already gathered around the rostrum, waiting for the speech of our leader. We feel the tension crackling in the air. Everything is too quiet and silent.

— Hi Adrian. I didn't expect to see you at this time.

— Neither do I, but Anton let me go me until sunrise.

— Your vampire is one of the strangest. Why does he never eat before going to the castle? No bloodsucker can stop eating except him.

My best friend is right. Anton is a very special vampire. First of all, nobody knows what his function is with the vampire king. He goes to the castle from sunset, sometimes until dawn, but none of the servants know why he is there and his visits to the vampire king are the only ones to be done behind closed doors. Besides, this story of not drinking blood before going there makes it even weirder. I do not doubt for a moment that depriving him of food causes him physical suffering. Yet he never deviates from that rule. One might think he feeds at the castle, but that is rarely to happen. He generally waits until he finds me to hunt together, both of us. The arrival of our leader on the stage interrupted my thoughts. Dumitru is the oldest werewolf in the pack, the firstborn, and our supreme leader regardless of what the vampire king thinks. We sincerely obey him and we have sworn loyalty to him until death. In fact, the death which has already happened to some of us.

— Good evening, everyone. I won't keep you waiting or give you a long speech. My brothers, it is time to act and free ourselves from our chains now and forever for all of us. We have been slaves of vampires for too long. We will act tomorrow night to gain our freedom.

Is it that early ? It seemed to me that he had just begun to eliminate the weakest and the least effective vampires in the kingdom to reduce Zoran's army.

— Why haste ? There are still many vampires.

One of my comrades asked loudly the question that everyone asks. A few weeks ago, we all decided that our freedom must be earned and not to be under the vampires' domination anymore. Only a coup takes time and requires the organization. Some of my comrades already began to free themselves from their vampiric trio by exterminating them without attracting attention. However, many of us are still at the service of at least two vampires and their power play. Moreover, their exceptional strength and regeneration could cause our loss. It's true that we are powerful, but not as much as vampires.

— Would you question my decisions, Ivan?

Dumitru jumps from the podium where he was perched and stands right in front of the young wolf. Ivan is one of the last born of the pack. He's only forty years old and the vampires he serves are rather kind towards him, exactly as Anton. So, he doesn't feel the urgency of the situation. This is not the case neither for all the werewolves, and certainly nor for our leader whose angry tone clacks in the night air.

— It's definitely not, Dumitru. I just think ...

Our leader grabs him by the throat and lifts him above the ground, cutting off his breathing.

— You are not asked to think. The pack has been suffering for too long under the yoke of these murderers. I'm getting tired of us being the villains in history.

Too many deaths, too many massacres. We have been doing the dirty work of vampires for two centuries. And for this sole purpose we were created by Zoran himself. We are the guardians of the vampire king. Our duty is exterminating humans bitten by vampires to prevent their transformation. Zoran did so in order to put an end to the untimely increase of his people without having to get his hands dirty. He did not want to bend down to finish his own meals. Protecting the castle all day is also one of our duties. Since vampires are the most vulnerable as they are confined inside, with no way to escape in case of danger. He just forgot that wolves are by nature wild. Some of our people have already tried to escape to live differently, but Zoran tracked them down so easily and eliminated them to the last man; thus, making them an example to other lycanthropes who would tempt to do the same.

Dumitru releases Ivan who collapses down to the ground, taking a steady breath after some laborious inspirations.

— The vampire king is preparing to flee after his losses and the desertion of humans in the region. The only choice he will have is to leave his castle. It will be a unique opportunity for us to capture him and make him confess how he created us.

Dumitru has been looking for the secret of our creation for two hundred years without any significant progress. He did some research. He integrated into the human world to learn every single thing related to genetics. But he unsuccessfully didn't manage to create a werewolf. At one point, he even believed that vampire blood was flowing through our veins, but it turns out that our lycanthrope nature violently rejects the venom of vampires. The thing that caused paralysis and excruciating pain to our body for days. This is a very common way of punishing us in vampires' compound. I've never paid for it. The only vampire I serve is Anton and he has always been so kind and respectful to me. A rare commodity among vampires who most often consider us as a sub-race. Our leader has long wanted to increase our numbers to provide relative protection against any attack through numerical superiority. He also thinks that it is a specific feature in our blood that allows Zoran to easily find the deserters of the pack. It has never been a question of capture, but of killing. Why this turnaround? Something is going on.

After an hour of talking about which strategy to adopt, each werewolf goes back to his business. We agreed upon keeping our habits without any change so as not to arouse even more the suspicions of the vampire king. For my part, I have a few hours left before I have to find Anton. I take this occasion to go see Dumitru. Like Ivan, I find it curious to embark on a war for which we are neither ready nor able. I walk into our leader's house without knocking. One of my privileges. We have known each other for nearly a hundred and fifty years and have been friends for as long as I can remember. As a result, I became his second and I do not understand why he did not keep me informed of his plan earlier.

— I suspected that you would come to see me.

After a hug, I take the time to check my friend who is changed a lot. He becomes more tired than usual. In fact, being at Zoran's personal service has been wearing him down for so long. If I were him, I'm not sure I would have survived more than a century without going crazy.

— What's going on, Dumitru? I know you well enough to know that you wouldn't risk an attack on Zoran without a good reason.

His deep sigh does not bode good things. I have never seen my friend so tired and so defeated.

— You are right, Adrian. I have to admit that I am putting my personal interests ahead of those of the pack for once, but I will not apologize and nothing will change my mind. I'm running out of time.

— What do you mean ?

Certainly, He has been working in secret for years, to protect our people from Zoran's madness putting his safety in the back. Sometimes he provokes the Vampire King's wrath. How are things different today?

— I'm dying, Adrian.

— What ? It's impossible !

— Look at me closely, brother.

I concentrate on his face and then pick up what disturbed me at first: wrinkles have appeared at the corners of his eyes and I see discreet white hair among his thick black locks. Signs of aging in the same way as humans.

— You are getting old.

— Yes, absolutely. I am the oldest lycanthrope in the pack and we mistakenly assumed that we were immortal like vampires since none of us showed signs of old age. That is not the case. Time catches up with me and my end comes quickly. Every day, I feel a little more of my strength abandoning me. Our decline begins probably after our two hundred years and it is much more precipitous than for humans.

Then I understand why he wants to quickly launch the offensive and capture Zoran.

— You hope to counteract the effects of aging by learning the secrets of our birth.

— Yes. Zoran has always been a master of our destiny for far a long time. And I would not allow him to be a master of my death. Why would these monsters roam the earth indefinitely without any respect for life when we would only have two hundred years? Two hundred years of slavery, what's more. I've been thinking about my revenge for more than a century. It's high time to act and take our revenge. If I have to leave this Earth, it will not be alone. I intend to drag the sharp teeth into my fall.

Indeed, Dumitru has been brooding over his reprisals since the death of his blood brother a hundred and fifty years earlier. Andrej died under mysterious conditions and Dumitru never accepted it. The wolf was my predecessor to Anton and I'm sure the vampire had nothing to do with this arbitrary execution. Or at least, he never gave me a reason to think differently. Our leader is convinced that his brother was killed because he saw something at the castle that he shouldn't have seen. Consequently, they shut him up. I do not think that this is a sufficient reason to risk the lives of our comrades by acting without thinking.

— We could take the time to develop a stronger plan…

His groaning voice echoes in the room.

— NO.

He is taking up a calmer tone, which in no way removes the virulence of his remarks.

— I wouldn't die because of the vampire king. We will capture him and make him reveal to us the secrets of our existence even if I have to make him suffer for hours for it. And then I'd kill him after I tortured him to the height of his black soul.

I realize at this moment that he's scared. Afraid of

death. A death that he can do nothing against. Our leader is strong. One does not remain at the service of a tyrant for two centuries without hardening himself. He always wanted to control everything related to the punishments inflicted by the vampires on the leadership of the pack. However, he can do nothing against the time that passes and that steals his life. He can't fight time himself.

— Will you support me?

— As always. But I want to talk about the trap again. I do really understand your thirst to live but it won't be to the detriment of our brothers' lives.

He nods slowly, realizing that he is crossing the line.

— Will you be my safeguard if madness awaits me?

— I can put you in your place if necessary, but I'm sure you won't give me any reason to do so.

— Who knows? The approach to death changes everything. I wish you never see this torment. I'll make sure that it never happens to you.

Finally, my discussion with Dumitru leaves me sad and depressed. These words run around my head on my way to Anton. I have to meet him at the foot of the castle so he can feed himself and I can finish the poor bastard who served him food before he was reborn as a vampire. Our leader is determined in his quest, but his personal reasons take precedence over the common good. He thinks collateral damage is acceptable. I do strongly disagree with that. His health conditions must not make the death of any of us acceptable. Furthermore, attacking Zoran head on is a sheer madness. It's a death sentence for the wolf that will be captured, and the same thing for the whole pack. If we do not succeed, nothing can stop the vampire king from killing us until the last one. All he has to do is recreate younger, more obedient werewolves, like Ivan. Undoubtedly, I am certain that Zoran will have eaten before leaving his home and his strength is much greater than ours. It is also faster and more devious. The only occasion we will be left with is to capture him just before sunrise, where he will be most vulnerable. The sun is the vampires' biggest enemy, before us and our desire for freedom. UV rays are fatal to them. In his search for shelter to spend the day, the vampire king may be less attentive to his surroundings. This would allow us to capture him alive. Because the difficulty is there. It would be so easy to attack him numerously and tear his throat without waiting or hesitating. But that's not our goal, because if he dies, we won't get the answers we need to survive.

Lost in the midst of all these ideas and battle plans, I realize that I arrived at the meeting point by guessing on the ground the gigantic shadow of the place guardian. The silhouette of the three-headed stone dragon is really enormous. There is a legend that talks about it. By the way, Russia is full of legends, some concerning me. Myths about werewolves and vampires are passed down from one generation to another. But I like most that one of the dragons. It's about the dragon Zmeï Gorynytch, guardian of the Kalinov Bridge, the only access to Zoran Castle and which marks the border between life and death, was defeated by a brave knight with a pure heart who came to free a princess held prisoner. Legend says it that the horrible fire-breathing dragon will come back to life when a princess needs him and a soul of such extraordinary blood as his murderer comes before him to ask for his assistance. Actually, I prefer this story to that one about werewolves in the surrounding villages. We are described as soul devourers, cannibals and monsters of the underworld. certainly, there is not that soul pure enough to awaken the legendary dragon and make it appear. I don't know what the blind windows of the castle are hiding in the background of the statue, but nothing good can remain with the vampire king, the greatest murderer of the Middle Ages.

Chapter 3

Tatjana

My mind is boiling, I prepare myself unconvincingly. I am thinking about a war. My father said that a war was going to be raging on our doorstep. Werewolves call for their independence. I have had the displeasure to propose to negotiate with their leader. I rub my cheek, which is still sensitive after the huge slap this idea brought on me.

« We do not negotiate with dogs. They are nothing more than garbage. They swallow our garbage and stand guard. That is the only purpose of their existence. They have no leader. Their only master is me, and it is time to remind them of that. I'm already giving them too much freedom. I'm going to fix it. Instead of thanking me, they want to overthrow me. I will crush their desire to revolt and everything will come back to normal. »

No wonder they want to break free from their chain because of the little consideration that the king gives them. After the life he had that led him to his death, one would think that he would have learned from the mistakes of others. That is not true, when I was younger, I had a hard time accepting this life of confinement. I asked him why he kept me locked up at the castle. He then told me about his own birth to supposedly open my eyes to the darkness of the world.

«Listen to me, Tatjana. I was born at a time of the jungle law, when the strongest reigned. I was at the service of Lord Vladimir, a rich man, very high placed with the tsar. He reigned over all our land with an iron hand, and woe to him who dared to stand up to him. I was one of his servants, or rather, his slave. I had to collect tithes in the surrounding villages. The villagers hated me. Every time I made my rounds, they slammed the door in my face, spat at me, or threw their trash in my face. I was synonymous with suffering for them, hard work for a miserable salary. They had nothing and I took everything from them in the name of Vladimir. One day, I came back to the castle with less money than expected because the locals had no more. Nevertheless, instead of attacking his subjects, Vladimir cut off my ear as punishment, because I should have found a solution to make the wretched pay their debts in one way or another. Then I had to remove all women of childbearing age in payment of their debt. Suffice to say that they hated me all the more. I destroyed their family. I was taking the poor women to the castle for Vladimir's pleasure. I didn't do it out of choice or cruelty, but it didn't make any difference to them. »

I was horrified by Zoran's actions. I thought then that he should have resisted. He should have helped those poor people. Of course, he guessed my fear.

« Don't look at me that way, Tatjana. You don't know what sacrifice we're willing to make to survive. Every time I tried to protect those who did not hesitate to strike me with their contempt, I paid the price. »

He then showed me his tongue pierced in the center and his hands with missing phalanxes. I went through hard times to realize that the Middle Ages was totally different time in everything. While I was living sheltered from the world, in total self-sufficiency. Yet, I was not at the end of the horrific tale of his rebirth.

« Then, there was no more woman or money to recover. I could not take the men to him as they had to work in the fields and I was reluctant to take the children to Vladimir. I still had a bit of a conscience. So, I tried to reason the Lord and make him see my reason. That was my last mistake, the fatal one to me, indeed. »

My father never shows pain or compassion, but the suffering that had transversed in his voice was the first time. These are my father's reflexes of the weak unlike Zoran who is not weak. I brought him trouble.

« Vladimir knew my greatest fear and he used it against me. In the Middle Ages, the woods were invaded by wild wolves that came out at nightfall looking for food. I couldn't bear to hear them howl at death. Vladimir tied me up outside the compound and left me at their mercy. Those scavengers devoured me alive while I screamed with all might. »

Zoran had tensed his fingers on the armrests of his armchair, a terror mask on his face, reliving the worst moment of his human life. Then I had a gesture of compassion for him. I had put my hand on his arm as a sign of support and felt hollows and bumps through the fabric. Then, he escaped my touch suddenly.

« I woke up amidst the excrement of the castle's rich people. My remains had been thrown into the dung pit as if I were not worth more than that, without any respect to the person I had been. Can you just imagine what I felt when I woke up half-puffed, the pain and stench still sticking to my skin shreds? »

To be clear, I really couldn't imagine that. I lived in autarky, I had no memory of my human life and I did not know any kind of suffering. Loneliness and rejection are my daily portion. Even though Zoran has already inflicted physical abuse on me, I don't know what it's like to be betrayed by my own people or to be tortured to the point of wishing to die.

« I went to the nearest village to ask for help. When they saw me, they all scream out loud claiming that I was a monster from hell. There I was, half of my body, devoured and bloodied, by wolves, in front of them. Unfortunately, instead of giving me a helping hand, they threw me away again. »

He had smiled in a way as an icy shiver went up my spine and bristled with little hair on the back of my neck. Insanity had taken its place in the depths of his dead eyes.

« The thirst for blood overpowered me. I bit every one of them all. I felt delighted with every drop of blood I drained of them. I really enjoyed killing them all, even the children. I was a little disappointed when they finally got up a few hours later. I did not expect it. At that time, I did not know the power of the venom contained in my canines. Fortunately, the sunrise burned most of them and taught me that I should be wary of UV rays! »

Not only there was no intention of remorse in his voice, but on the contrary he was very satisfied.

« The next night, my first disciples who had mistreated me the least and to whom I had decided to let alive were lucky that I took them with me. We had fun at the castle. After all, I had a little visit to Vladimir and his vassals to thank them for this second life that was granted to me thanks to them. »

His canines had descended under the blow of emotion to this memory. Obviously, it's a very happy memory for the monster that sleeps inside him.

« I took pleasure in gutting him, draining him of his blood and flaying him, so that he could taste the joy of waking up with atrocious suffering. Then, once he was transformed, I ripped out his throat with my teeth. »

I feel nauseous just thinking about it. It's weird, how can anyone be excited about the memory of a massacre like that?

« I'm putting you away from the inevitable disappointment of the world. »

After his explanation, I realized that I would never be accepted just as he never was. And this had left me perplexed as well as deeply hurt.

Today, it leaves me mostly in the dark. It was persecution and the top desire for revenge that led to his transformation into a vampire. However, he inflicts the same fate on werewolves and hopes for a different reaction from them. It's idealistic and unrealistic.

— You are anxious, Tatjana.

Anton has not left me since my father's announcement. He does worry about me. Honestly, this moment is what I dreamt of all my life, but the circumstances in which I realized it spoiled and messed my happiness. And the least I can say is that, these circumstances are really weird and frightening.

— Everything is fine.

Anton approaches me from behind and plays with a strand of my hair, dragging it between his pale fingers.

— You're a terrible liar, princess. You're good at hiding your nature by omitting information.

However, you betray yourself every time you open your mouth.

Saying that, he taps my lower lip with his index finger. I sigh in frustration. He's right. It's true that I am not competent in acting, and Anton knows me too well to be deceived.

— What's wrong with you?

I fall with all my weight on my bed. What's wrong with me? Actually, my whole life is bothering me. Two hundred years of aimless existence and a vampiric nature that doesn't match my state of mind. Who was I before my transformation? Zoran never wanted to tell me. He assures me that it doesn't matter, that my life began the day he found me. But found me where? I'm not sure it's so trivial, and all this adds up to my many other questions. However, my friend is waiting for my answer, and all he can think of is our last conversation with the king.

— Why should I stay away from the castle if the danger is as close as he thinks it is? Wouldn't I be safer by his side, surrounded by our people?

I can see that Anton doesn't understand my father's decision any more than I do. He rubs his beard on his pointed chin while I look at him, and then he finally breathes a deep sigh as he squats down in front of me.

— I don't know, Tatjana. You know very well that Zoran's instructions are not to be discussed and that he only gives the information he deems necessary. All I can assure you is that I won't let you out of my sight for a second. I will follow you like a shadow.

Anton has always had a weakness for me. He even kissed me once, but I feel nothing like that towards him. He doesn't make my near-dead heart beat harder or faster. I should probably stop reading romance books of the human world. However, I hope that one day a man will mean as much to me as I mean to him and that he will wake me up from my slow agonistic life.

- I've lost you again, Princess.

My friend's icy hand on my cheek startled me, and I came back to conscience. He smiled at me, a smile that I did feel.

— You will never lose me. You are my best friend.

He looks into my eyes for some time then he nods his head with a sorrowful look on his face.

— Anyway, you need to finish packing. Be ready by the sunset and don't overload yourself. We'll be on our way without delay.

— Where will we go?

— We'll go to East. There's a small village that the vampires have never visited before. Humans should not distrust us. We'll spend the day there in the shelter before continuing on a little further, to an empty dwelling the king has indicated to me.

That's sounds pretty well and good, but it's a problem, and not the least of which is the fact that it's a problem.

- Anton, how will you feed yourself?

For me, I can eat anywhere without attracting attention. We'll always manage to find a small animal for me to feed on. However, Things are getting complicated for my friend. He needs human blood. He doesn't want to do without it anyway. Also, he's forbidden to take his wolf with him and turning a human into a vampire is definitely not a choice...

— Don't worry about that. I can go without blood for a few days.

I grab his arm.

— Don't do that. You know very well that this will certainly make you sick and weak.

He delicately puts his index finger on my lips to

shut me up.

— Everything is going to be all right, Tatjana. It's only a matter of three or four days. It won't take Zoran much longer to restore calm to the pack and I'm willing to make any sacrifice for you.

He kisses the corner of my lips gently and leaves the room without a glance back, leaving me standing there with my mouth open.

The latest events have really made me be struck. I amazingly realize that Anton's feelings towards me are not disappeared at all. I even think that they have only grown over the last fifty years since the day he admitted his feelings of love. I thought he had forgotten. But it's not true; and now I fear the worst. I would not want him to put himself in danger because of me. I am tempted to go back to the Vampire King either to ask him for the favor of staying by his side, or to have a bodyguard other than Anton for my trip, at worst. Nevertheless, I know in advance that this is a bad idea and a waste of time. My first idea will bring me about his contempt. And the second one will raise too many questions that would risk Anton a severe punishment. Whatever I do, I'm at an impasse, a dead-end. Therefore, I carry out the orders of the two men in my life with a terrible sadness and confusing thoughts running around my mind, looking for a better solution. Then I slip into my satin sheets to sleep hoping to find some rest and relax before the radical change in my life.

Chapter 4

Adrian

Anton is too late. He arrives just before the first rays of sunshine start to appear in the distance. He throws me his last lunch without even looking at me. He has obviously been relentless in his pursuit of the poor man who falls into my arms, as soft as a disarticulated puppet. There's never been such a lack of restraint with humans in normal times. I carry out my duty in silence, without even feeling sorry for the fate of the poor human, while he is already walking away, and I hurry up to throw the dead body in a pit provided for that purpose. Unlike the popular legend that says we devour humans like cannibals. It's not quite true, this rarely happens. But, after all Lycanthropes are wolves. We prefer to hunt game. So, we simply tear the dead to pieces to prevent their rebirth and then set them on fire when daylight comes.

I team up with my partner in a few steps, but I am disturbed by his contempt.

— Anton ? You got a problem? Right?

Anton is staring at me with unusual colder gaze, if black eyes can express anything else, but I have always managed to distinguish a similar emotion in his eyes even if they are black. Actually, they have never seemed so dead and empty.

— None. You've always served me well. Why would there be a problem?

I feel a bad annoyance compressing my stomach. A doubt oversteers me after hearing his cold tone, just as his eyes are. Maybe my partner isn't as peaceful as I thought, and the rumors in the pack about Andrej's death are less far-fetched than I thought.

— Was your visit to the castle so bad?

He stops and stares deeply at me. It makes me uncomfortable and my fingers stretch out in claws under stress. I don't understand this change of events. Does the Vampire distrust the loyalty of werewolves? It's a possibility. Yet there hasn't been a collective call-up of vampires to organize a war, the fact contradicts that hypothesis. On the other hand, Zoran believes himself to be almighty and invincible. He's quite capable of imagining himself against a pack of wolves. What annoys me most is that he has no intention of leaving his castle while

Dumitru is convinced that he must leave. I think something wrong is happening. I'm breathing deeply through my nose to recover my normal shape. I really don't wish to provoke the wrath of the only vampire I think I can trust.

— What are you thinking about, Adrian? Is it your next betrayal?

I swallow my saliva sideways in the face of this direct accusation and get defensive. Eventually, my confidence in him breaks down in seconds. A potential danger lies in all my senses.

— I've never hurt you.

— Yes, never. But what about the wolves of vampires who were found murdered lately, is this the fate you keep for me?

He's right. The betrayal didn't come from Anton, but indirectly from me. So, Zoran has heard about the murders and knows the investigators. That's not exactly a surprise. Zoran knows almost everything. What is surprising is that he hasn't yet reacted accordingly while he was in a hurry to exterminate all deserters as soon as they escaped. The first vampire was killed a fortnight ago and the werewolf killer is free as air, walking around the pack as if nothing had happened. Normally Zoran kills the rebel werewolves the night after their misdeed. Fifteen of our own should have died at the rate of one kill a day. I'd rather reassure Anton that he won't be the first to lose his life.

— You've never given me any reason to distrust you or even think to hurt you. You are as courteous vampire as they come.

— So, you're one of the few werewolves who want to start a rebellion against my people? Glad to hear it!

I prefer to keep calm and silent rather than betray the pack. Anton is frustrated, I can see it in his face. He interprets my silence as a confession, which is deeply the case.

— It's clear. Then I'll be dispensing with your services from now on. I wouldn't want to have my throat ripped out by a man I considered my best and faithful friend.

I didn't expect this rejection and I'm taking it harder than I thought. An unspoken trust had finally been taking place between us.

— Anton, you need me and it's my duty to...

— With Zoran's agreement, I'm releasing you from your duties.

I can't answer anything after that. Nobody can question an order from the Vampire King unless you want to suffer the consequences. However, I am sorry for the situation. Anton's right, we've developed a certain friendship over the decades and it's a hard break. Only, my pack comes first. I swore an oath since my birth and I am not willing to deny it for a vampire, not even for Anton who doesn't deserve my hatred for his people.

— Which vampire do I serve from now on?

Anton goes on his way without giving me a look back.

— I don't know. I have no idea. Zoran will summon you tomorrow to find out. Be at his disposal on time, otherwise prepare to regret it. That is not my concern anymore.

There's no need to insist. It's quite clear that Anton wants nothing more to do with me. He simply dismisses me with a wave of his hand, like a dog. He has never considered me so. I do really understand the anger of my people against this bellicose posture. But I can't blame him at all.

— Goodbye, Anton. Take care of yourself.

He shrugs his shoulders and I stare at his back as he goes to the little house, he occupies about a hundred meters from the castle to spend the day there.

I'm not on guard outside the castle today to ensure the safety of its inhabitants while sleeping. My last conversation with Anton is a warning, it alarms me. I'd like to discuss this with Dumitru and revise our plan. I think Zoran is hiding his next step well since he apparently hasn't taken any reaction against the massacres of his people yet. I'm sure he suspects everything. So, if we attack the king now, we're riding for a fall, for a disaster. Most of the wolves have taken their posts around the vampire houses for the day and the pack quarters are almost empty. The sun is already high in the sky when I cross them. Unlike vampires, we can tolerate UV rays without any problem and I enjoy the warmth that embraces my skin. The alpha's house is empty, without any signal of his presence. It is rare that he is not there during the day and I didn't have any idea of him being away today. I end up coming across Ivan in the forest bordering our den. The young wolf has two black eyes and a slinging arm, a sullen and downcast look on his bruised face.

— Ivan ? Did your vampire attack you?

His contemptuous gaze strikes me. And then the sadness opens doors leading me to anger.

— The vampire I serve is less devious than ours. At least the bloodsuckers attack from the front. And afterwards, we call ourselves better than them! They've never done anything to me!

I'm confused and refuse to understand his innuendo.

— What are you talking about? Wolves don't fight each other. Dumitru keeps an eye on that.

Ivan's skin undulates and gradually becomes covered with grey hairs before regaining a smooth and hairless appearance. The metamorphosis is being motivated by the anger and the young wolf is obviously struggling against it

— Dumitru threw his own rules behind, in the garbage. He certainly didn't like me speaking in front of the pack and he made me understand this with his fists just before being called by Zoran. I hope the Vampire King will give him a knockdown. Dumitru is not better than Zoran.

I can't blame Ivan for thinking so. The vampire he serves has never punished him, unlike our Alpha. However, Dumitru never used his fists to make his word heard. He had always preferred to have discussion and argumentation with the pack, especially with young werewolves who are unwilling to risk their lives to get their freedom when their life in the service of vampires does not yet weigh on them.

— Obviously Dumitru is tense, and it's not an excuse, but...

— You're right, there's no reason to worry about his mistreat. He's changed a lot. I guess Zoran's behavior has rubbed off on him. Now, if you don't mind, I'm going to stretch my legs and get better.

— Yes, sure.

Ivan removes the fabric that supports his arm and his limbs lie down in a clacking sound. His phalanges shorten and become covered with pale grey down while his nails turn into claws. His nose becomes longer, his mouth takes the shape of a mouth where impressive teeth take place in a powerful jaw. The muscles in his thighs swell and the tendons start to emerge until becoming two robust hind legs. Although Ivan is still young, he clearly has a strong and an impressive werewolf character as well as a perfect combination of wolf and man. Our build is similar to that of a human with muscles developed like those of a wolf, and our body is covered with fur, but we have the human posture. We walk straight on our hind legs, except when we hunt, where we are faster by leaning on our four limbs. Furthermore, we heal faster when we metamorphose. And that's why Ivan has just transformed. After hearing a wolf howl, he rushes into the depths of the forest, leaving me behind, without answer. Then, a discomfort is growing in my heart.

I didn't even think to ask him why Zoran requested Dumitru's presence. Normally, the vampire king refuses the presence of the pack inside the castle when the sun rises. The Vampire King is cautious and knows he is vulnerable during the day. So, he needs our protection, but we necessarily must stay outside. Bringing the Alpha into the devil's lair at this hour is the beginning and certainly not a coincidence. It confirms my suspicions. The Vampire King has his doubts, and this compromises our plans. Unless it was just to prepare for his escape that he requested Dumitru's presence. It would make sense that our alpha would be on the trip if Zoran is really planning to get out of the castle. It would be an additional opportunity for a successful attack and we could receive the information directly. Well, it's unnecessary to rack my brain until Dumitru comes back. It's better as well getting some rest. It's going to be a long and stormy night ahead, and I'll need to be fully prepared and be able to possess all my resources to carry out the plan.

Finally, I manage to get some sleep, having too much on my mind, and I wake up with a start of dusk. I stretch my aching limbs in an uncomfortable position and take time to admire the landscape. I love the orange and pinkish colours that the sunset brings out among the trees. I can't think of anything more beautiful in life. Vampires don't know what they're missing by only going out after dark. At the same time, watching the sunset view would be their last pleasure. They'd get fried by the UV rays. It takes my mind back to Anton. He was so strange and unusual. Did King Zoran confide in one of his oldest lieutenants about a possible rebellion of the lycanthropic pack, which would explain his mistrust of me? Perhaps he even had a role to play in the king's escape, which would explain my distance. Although I never gave him any reason to doubt my loyalty. Zoran's innuendoes must have dissatisfied him so much and weakened his position with the king. Anton is evidently disappointed with me. He must have felt betrayed, although I was not the planner of the war which was about to begin. Hmm that's nonsense. Why would Zoran have asked Dumitru for help in this case? It's no secret that despite Zoran's arrogance, he can't ignore the fact that Dumitru is our leader in the pack. All this doesn't make any reason. Besides, when I see that Dumitru hasn't returned all day, my anxiety grows. His disappearance is more than worrying, and it calls into question our whole strategy. I can't risk an attack without knowing what happened to our alpha and I have no contact inside the castle since Anton has fired me. I'm doomed to wait for Zoran's summons so that I can snoop behind the closed castle gates. That's really annoying situation. I'm second in command to the alpha, his beta. If I were to disappear, the pack would be left leaderless and defenseless against the vampires. Perhaps that was the Vampire King's plan? To weaken the pack so he could take back control of the lycanthrope without exterminating us all. But mercy is not in the king's jargon! I'm gnawing at my brakes as I await the call that will probably change our future.

Chapter 5

Tatjana

I restlessly turn and roll over in my bed, and this compresses my heart and makes cold sweats rise up my spine. I feel like I've been hearing screaming for several hours, which may be true, by the way. Sometimes human's screams, and other times those of agonizing wild beast. The screams echoed throughout the castle and froze the blood in my veins, keeping my eyes wide open and my soul in pain all day long. This is not the first time this has happened. I do strongly know Zoran's bloodthirsty character. I still remember when a man came into my room without permission. I never knew who he was or what he wanted, but I can still hear his cries of pain as the Vampire King punished him for no more than the simple act of seeing me. I saw this scene by chance a long time ago. He didn't wait until he was in his quarters to shove his hand into his chest and rip his heart out, with a Machiavellian look on his face. It had taken me days to clean the blood off the floor and I had cried for the first time in my life. I still feel as if the spirit of that man haunts me and accuses me of being the reason for his death, until today. At least this time I am not responsible for the torture Zoran inflicted. That doesn't make it any more comfortable. I feel like I'm connected to this battered creature and feel every pain inflicted upon him. I am a peaceful vampire who only wants to live in peace with the world around me and I am very far from that goal. I fear that I will never achieve my goal by staying with Zoran. So, I welcome Anton's arrival with a little too much enthusiasm. To be honest, I literally throw myself at him, hugging him with all my strength and finally managing to ignore the whip cracking and the screams that they created.

— It's all right, princess.

Anton gives me back a hug by caressing my back top-down with exaggerated slowness. Then I realize that this gesture does not mean the same to him as it does to me, it's possible. The sparkling glow in his bottomless irises when I take a step back confirms this to me and I choose to explain my gesture before he misunderstands me.

— I just had a terrible night.

My friend gives me a dazzling smile from his scarlet lips, a sign that he fed before he came. I'm too upset to hold it against him, especially since we don't know when his next meal will be.

— It's no problem. I'll comfort you as much as you like.

Finally, I let him go after a shy smile.

— Let's get out of here.

He shakes his head and gives me a crystal glass.

— Not until you've fed. It's going to be a long night. We have a long walk ahead of us before we can settle down to sleep.

Definitely, being a vampire doesn't just have its perks. We can't live in the zeitgeist since technology, just like mechanics, do not work well with us. In other words, cars full of electronics don't like us the same as old cars with simple engines do. Everything breaks down as soon as we get close!!! The only advantage in this fact, according to Anton, is that humans can't kill us with their modern machine because it doesn't work in our presence. Moreover, the same thing goes with the guns and other similar joyous things too, they get damaged as we approach. As far as I'm concerned, I don't see the point of it, since being locked up in a castle all the time, I risk nothing. The only exception to this rule is mobile phones. Of course, not the latest versions I've seen in magazines, but the oldest clamshell models with big buttons that made communication between werewolves and vampires so much easier, again according to Anton.

I take the container from my friend's hands and carry it to my lips. However, I stop before I drink a drop. The smell is not familiar, it's not the same as usual. It's copperier, more caustic.

— What animal is for breakfast tonight?

He refuses to answer me and lifts the glass to force me to drink. Anton has always preferred to keep his mouth shut rather than lie to me. I dodge his grip and I throw the bowl at the other end of the room, pouring liquid over white marble.

— I don't want to drink human blood, I refuse it. I've already told you. We've already discussed this, and you've accepted my choice. You've always kept your word by bringing me the blood of an animal. Why did you want to deceive me?

As a result, his anger transcends mine surprising me with his fierce tone.

— Very simply, because we're not going for a cakewalk. You're risking your life on the outside and you need to be fully at your top power in case of an attack. It's time you realized what kind of world we live in. Wake up! this isn't one of your novels!

He had never raised his voice in front of me until now and I realize that he is much more worried than he has let me see so far. He nervously closes and opens his hands to control his mood. It touches me, but without changing anything.

— I won't deny my beliefs out of fear. If it is to be my only and last journey, then it will be my last and only journey. Nevertheless, I would die with my head held high and without killing anyone. Is that clear or are we going to have to argue until you listen to reason?

Anton exhales noisily and places his forehead against mine, eyes tightly together.

— You exhaust me, Tatjana. I adore you, but sometimes you arouse my anger. Fortunately, I know you well enough to have foreseen your reaction.

He's getting up and going to get a second drink in the corridor next to my quarters. He hands it to me, resigned.

— I was just hoping to change your mind. Just this time.

I sniff the drink, suspicious, but don't smell anything fishy. Just an attractive smell that makes my stomach growl with envy.

— You can drink it all. I promise this is not another trap. There's only woodcock blood fresh from the day.

I look at him for a moment and try to guess the deception on his marble face, but I see nothing of that. Only impatience with my reticence on his too smooth and too perfect face.

— OK. I trust you. However, don't ever try to force me to drink human blood again. Never.

He tries to reason with me while I deliciously sip my drink.

— You're the only vampire on the planet who can drink cold blood from a glass that doesn't come straight out of a warm vein; and you don't even use it to make a human blood supply that you could drink without having to hunt every day. You really don't know how lucky you are. If I were you, I'd stockpile it in the fridge without having to kill a human every time. That's the problem with vampires: We don't know how to stop once our fangs are immersed in soft, juicy flesh.

I am just imagining myself hunting a poor

defenseless creature to empty it of its essence while hearing its heart slowing down with each suck makes me nauseous. I really don't have the courage to finish my drink and put it back half full on my bedside table, before I vomit it all up. I'm really bad predator. I wonder, if it was just me to exist, the locals wouldn't have to worry about their safety at all. But anyway, I would probably starve to death after a few days, unable to catch an innocent little beast. In short, without Anton, I would be completely lost. He's essential to my survival and I'm well aware of that.

— All of it. You have to drink it all, princess. I told you, you need to gain strength.

He obstinately provides me with that damn drink again, which I'm resisting. I throw it in his face. In books, princesses do whatever they want and give orders, and not receiving them, as my case, within these walls. I reluctantly swallow the rest of my meal and show my displeasure by smashing the glass on the table when I put it back. I sweep away the scattered pieces of glass with a wave of my hand while Anton raises an eyebrow at my mood swings. However, my frustrations are not over yet. On the contrary, it looks like my friend has decided to test my limits and tried to push me reach the peak.

— Put these dark glasses over your eyes.

—What for?

Just a «please» would undoubtedly make me more obedient. However, being asked in this authoritative manner, brings out my annoying side, which I can only express in his presence, and I give myself to joy.

— Because I'm asking you to do so. Put on those sunglasses and put that coat on by folding the hood over your face.

Grrr ! He just really irritates me. It's the question that the sunglasses bother me too much, I have rather good night vision, although again, it's nothing compared to Anton's. However, I want explanations for all this staging and my bodyguard is reluctant to give them to me. He raises his arms to the sky. There, now there are two of us to be overwhelmed.

— Your eyes are a little too conspicuous. They shine at night; I'll let you know. You'll admit that we're more discreet!

Yes, my eyes shine like two incandescent flames, I

know that. Maybe he thinks his two bottomless pits are more discreet?

— You're not wearing one!

— If you continue, I'll knock you out and drag you over my shoulder like a vulgar bag, Tatjana. It's up to you to choose how you want to travel.

I put myself on the defensive, ready to fight. He gave me a few self-defense courses decades ago. I know there is no way to compare; his strength is too superior to mine, but I can give him a hard time. Finally, before my inflexible attitude, he surrenders.

— Easy, tiger. My eyes will deter the unwelcome from seeking trouble. I'll hide them as we approach the village where we'll spend the day.

— What about the coat?

— We're about to cross paths with vampires and in case you've forgotten, female vampires aren't supposed to exist. I suppose you wouldn't want to attract the attention of a horny male.

I wince at this disturbing idea. Ugh.

— Horny? Vampires don't have that kind of thought every time they come across a woman, do they?

— This is no time for a vampire sex class,

princess. Simply put, vampires are men like any other, with needs and desires, and you're a beautiful woman who would definitely get their attention.

He slips his cold hand through my hair before helping me put on my long coat and wedging my hair under the hood.

— I thought I showed you the effect you have on men. On me, in particular.

Indeed, I did feel his erection rubbing against my lower belly the day he kissed me passionately, but I prefer not to dwell on this thought which bothers me to the utmost. I cannot consider Anton in this way, even though he is not charm with his protruding biceps between which I feel protected.

— I'm ready. We can go whenever you want.

He shakes his head, a smile on the corner of his lips.

— You drive me crazy, princess. Come on, let's go. It's already late and we can't afford to be any later otherwise, we'll be caught by the sun before we get there.

I nod and grab my backpack, which contains a few spares. Anton takes it from my hands and throws it on his back. Gentleman at all times.

— Let's hurry up. I hear commotion and I prefer that we meet as few people as possible before we leave the castle.

Above all, I see this welcome silence that rests my soul. The screams have finally stopped. Either the man is dead, a welcome greeting, or Zoran has grown tired for now and he will resume his work later, actually when I will no longer be there to hear him. Either way, I thank heaven for taking a break from the shouting.

Chapter 6

Tatjana

Anton was right. Undoubtedly, something unusual is going on at the castle: a meeting of vampires. We come across some of them in the corridors, looking at us with deep curiosity. Fortunately, they are obviously too nervous to linger on the fact that we are going in the opposite direction to theirs. I kept my head down, preventing anyone from seeing my face. As soon as we cross the main gate of the castle, I pause. I need a little time to realize where I am. I'm finally outside, free of my invisible chains. Suddenly the air seems purer, less polluted by the smell of dead bodies that floats through the building despite its cleanliness. The night is beautiful and I look at the sky to admire the twinkling stars that illuminate this dark picture of their beauty. Anton hooks my arm and takes a good step forward.

— I completely understand your curiosity, but the time is not for raptures. We must get as far away from the castle as possible before war breaks out.

This has the merit of bringing me back down to earth and I'm following him at the same pace.

— You seem convinced that events are about to unfold in a hurry. Why do you think that?

He squeezes his lips so tightly that they are only a thin line on his closed face.

— It's all right. As you wish. I've got all the time in the world, after all. I also would like to take a closer look at that statue.

Now, we are at the foot of an impressive three-headed colossus, as a statue. From my window, I could hardly imagine its size. I imagined it to be about no more than ten feet tall. In reality, it is actually four meters high and just as long from the tip of its tail to its pointed horns. Of course, I'm aware of the legend that runs over him. However, what really gives meaning to the myth which gives him an extraordinary power and strength is seeing him so close in reality. I feel so small at his feet and his paws. His two broad legs with sharp claws.

— Enough, Tat! Come on!

I tilt my head to the side.

— Tat ?

He comes closer to whisper in my ear, his breath

tickling my lobe.

— That sounds more masculine than Tatjana or Princess, don't you think?

— OK, OK. Now, tell me about the war that seems imminent.

— You're not going to let go and drag your feet until I tell you what's going on, are you?

— That's right. I'm willing to watch Zmei all night if I have to. I'd rather take the risk of you knocking me out than remain in the dark.

— And risk getting caught in the sunrise? Or that the trip would last longer and I'd starve to death?

— That's a cheap shot.

He knows I'd rather suffer a thousand deaths than be responsible for someone else's death. I set off again, completely ignoring him, strolling the air left and right to note the variations in the air and guess why.

— Are you going to ignore me all night?

I turn my head away from him.

— You behave like a child.

I'm holding back from sticking my tongue out at him. He'd be too happy to be right.

— A two hundred-year-old child, Tat! Don't you think that's strange?

No stranger than my presence in this forest, which takes on a gloomy air with the moon. Besides, I am a princess after all, I have the right to be capricious from time to time!

— You've won. I hate it when you're mad at me and you're stubborn as a mule! You're capable of ignoring me the whole trip and I couldn't stand it.

If I had known that just snubbing him was enough to get everything I want, I would have done it sooner.

— Zoran summoned his werewolf yesterday. He's the one you heard screaming.

I am not happy about this, but I do not see how this is an exceptional situation. It is certainly not the first time he has punished a lycanthrope he considers inferior to him.

— Dumitru is the first werewolf created by Zoran. He is also the alpha, the leader of the pack, although Zoran refuses to grant him this title, which he won out of loyalty and not out of oppression. In fact, the werewolf pack obeys Zoran out of obligation, but has sworn loyalty to Dumitru.

— Let me guess the rest. Zoran decided to beat

Dumitru to death to set an example for the other lycanthropes and discourage them from rebelling against the vampires.

He's shaking his head, tighter than ever

— You should have known the Vampire King since a long time. Zoran is more Machiavellian than that. It's never that simple. He doesn't want to establish his authority and risk another rebellion in a few decades. He definitely wants to break the resistance of the pack, as a whole. And there's only one way to do that.

I think I've guessed what he means by this, but I can't even pronounce an idea so bad that it brings tears to my eyes.

— There you go.

Anton wipes away a tear that escaped in spite of me and rolled down my cheek.

— Zoran captured the alpha to incite the rebels so as to reveal themselves, then he could exterminate them. The torture session is just a small bonus he gave himself. It's a way to prove to Dumitru who is the strongest. Although, I think, there's no worthiness in beating an enemy tied by unbreakable chains to a wall.

— He's going to commit genocide. Zoran will start

the war that threatens us.

— Yes. The most reckless lycanthropes will try to free Dumitru when they realize that Zoran has no intention of freeing him. Instead, Zoran's call to his wolf was just an ambush.

— And the vampires will kill them all.

Anton intertwines his fingers with mine as my heart is clutching by thinking of so many needless deaths. A simple power struggle when it would be enough for our two peoples to co-exist in harmony, without conflict.

— Zoran lures the werewolves into a trap and the alpha is used as bait. They have no chance of victory on the king's field.

— That's right. The king has summoned his most powerful and bloodthirsty vampires to make sure no enemy escapes. This is going to be a real slaughter.

I'm relieved I don't have to witness this massacre against my will.

— Thank you for taking me away from the castle.

— Don't thank me. It's not my decision and Zoran didn't do it for you. He just wants the werewolves to continue to ignore your existence.

— Wolves? And why wolves?

— I always thought Zoran was hiding vampires from me for some reasons. Why do you insinuate he's hiding lycanthropes from me?

My legitimate question seems to make him uncomfortable.

— Later on. We are approaching the village. Stay close to me and don't talk any more. I'll take care of everything.

Indeed, we are in front of typical houses view of the region as I can see from my window: wooden isbas similar to a cottage with a vegetable garden on the side. We are in a village of peasants where poverty can be seen in every broken road and very old cars. Anton puts on his glasses to camouflage his completely black eyes and leaves my hand. I feel so weak when I am away of his contact, but some remote areas of Russia are rather resistant and a gay couple would only attract unwelcome attention. We met almost no one on the way except for a few vampires, the only nocturnal creatures, who barely glanced at us before turning away, they recognize my friend. So, this is the first time I have ever met humans, without counting the only time I have fed on one of them, because thirst obscured and darkened my senses, as I don't even remember what my victim looked like. There are not many of them in the streets at this late hour, but there are a few of them staggering home, probably under the influence of alcohol. I carefully watch them. Probably a little too much.

— Tat, be more discreet. People don't like to be stared at insistently.

— I'm sorry.

I lower my head slightly towards the ground while continuing to look at them through my sunglasses. I find humans fascinating. However, regardless of how fascinating they are, all of them are similar to us. Same appearance, same posture. Even at this distance, I can hear their regular heartbeats. I can see the red rising to their cheeks. I even can guess the blood flowing in their veins and the warmth of their bodies, unlike the coldness of mine. Obsessed by my observation, I only realize that we have arrived at our destination when I hear Anton conversing with a woman of large stature and generous breasts standing behind a counter.

— Good evening, ma'am. We'd like a room for the night.

She's watching us with the same attention that I was watching earlier.

— The day is coming up soon and we don't rent rooms by the hour. We're not that kind of places. Besides, two men in the same room is not allowed in here.

Humans don't mince their words. With such a fragile appearance, I would have thought them more docile, less prone to conflict. Strangely enough, without Anton saying anything more, the woman goes back on her word.

— Of course, sir. As you wish.

I look up at the hostess, despite my friend's recommendations, and find that she doesn't even see me. Her eyes are haggard and dilated. I turn to Anton as he pulls his glasses up over his nose. What the hell is this mess? The woman hands us a key without even giving her money for the room.

— You're at number 11. It's the last door, left corridor. There are no customers next door, so you'll be quiet. Enjoy your stay with us, gentlemen.

She sits in her chair, still in the same catatonic state.

— What's the...

— Later on. Let's go to the bedroom. The sun comes up in an hour.

I'm fed up with all this secrecy. The journey has

just begun and I feel like I'm wading in ignorance. What bothers me the most is that I've always thought that Zoran is the only one who keeps information from me as well as knowing the reasons for my differences with the vampires. I suspect more and more that Anton also has the answers to these questions and that he has deceived me for far too long by keeping quiet. The vampire that I have considered my friend since birth has been lying to me, and probably spying for Zoran, all this time. I throw my things on the floor and take refuge in the bathroom before collapsing in tears like the nasty babes in my romantic novels.

— Tatjana, open up.

Certainly not, no. I need time to get my thoughts together and decide what I want in the future. I never thought I'd be thinking about giving Anton the wrong kind of company.

— Princess. Don't be childish.

— I'm taking shower before I go to bed. It's an adult behavior on the contrary.

I can hear his fingernails digging into the soft wood of the door.

— Hurry up! Wash up or I'm going to come over there and pull you out by your ass.

He's certainly capable of it. I go under the warm, soothing water and clean myself from all the dust and dirt caused by our long walk. The only problem is, in my rush, I didn't take my clothes to change, so I have to leave the room only wrapped in a very short towel. I put my head down and sneak under the sheets without even looking at him, covering myself up to my chin. Luckily, Anton stayed dressed, just lying over the blankets.

— Tatjana, I know you don't understand everything, but...

— I'm very tired. You can resume your lies tomorrow.

— My princess...

I turn my back on him, determined to ignore his useless pleas that will lead to nothing. I get tense when he sticks to my back and takes me in his arms, locking his grip firmly.

— Sleep well, Tatjana. I'm watching over you. Always.

It takes me a long time to sleep, feeling more betrayed than ever. He's not holding me against him out of affection, but to keep me from running away.

Chapter 7

Adrian

Dumitru still hasn't appeared yet, unlike other lycanthrope companions. They should be with their referent vampires, doing their duties, but they have hardly left at nightfall and are already returning. I can see two of them from very far, Vasile and Ivan. Ivan is now fully recovered from the punishment of our alpha. Perhaps they can give me some answers.

— Hey, guys. What are you doing here?

Vasile gives me a pat on the back saying hello.

— Our vampires were summoned to the castle and we are told to go home. We're not allowed to walk around that place until further notice.

What does it mean forbidden to do our duty? This is weird, it's not normal.

— Have you seen Dumitru ?

My friend frowns.

— No. Isn't he home already?

— No. Zoran summoned him in the morning and I

haven't heard anything about him since.

— Damn it. Do you think that ...

Hell yes! This whole thing reeks of entrapment. Only Zoran underestimates us. We're not idiots and we're not going to throw ourselves into the vampires' fangs with our heads down.

— He's using Dumitru to lure us into his lair and kill us in his territory.

Ivan sneers into his beard and starts to walk away.

— Don't rely on me to go and get myself slaughtered in the name of a revenge which I absolutely don't care about; It's not my concern. I am not in.

He's right and I completely understand that. I would never ask anyone to sacrifice their life by entering the castle under these mysterious conditions. But I still need a helping hand.

— Ivan, stay here.

He shows me the fangs and prepares to transform.

— Hey, take it easy, cub scout. I'm not going to send you to the slaughterhouse. However, we really need to know what's going on in the castle.

Ivan calms down and nods his head.

— I'll follow you, but I won't go there into the building, no matter what happens. Not even if we hear Dumitru screaming for help.

— That's fine with me. Vasile, are you in?

The werewolf looks at me with a raised eyebrow.

— Go snooping around the forest to spy on the bloodthirsty? Yeah! I'd love to. The crazier we are, the more we laugh.

Vasile... This werewolf is crazy. He has no self-preservation instincts. I'll have to keep an eye on him, otherwise we'll end up killed by his thoughtless and rashly actions.

We've been on a stakeout for less than fifteen minutes when I see Anton leaving the castle with a vampire whose face I can't see. It's unusual. All the other vampires have entered the building. He's the only one that got out. Him and this stranger. The situation is getting more and more inconsistent and there's no trace of Dumitru. I guess our alpha had a bad day. If he's still alive of course. Everything's possible.

— What's the next step? What do we do now? We go home, kill everyone and free Dumitru ?

I catch Vasile by the arm before he steps out of the canopy of the trees where we've been hiding.

— Don't say stupid things! There are at least fifteen of the oldest and most powerful vampires in there and there are only three of us.

— Only two, actually. I told you, I'm not going back into that castle.

— Yes, Ivan. I know.

Vasile resumes his plan.

— Then let's get some backup and come back strong.

I am shaking my head. No way.

— It's not necessary. We don't know the inside of the building. The pack would be exterminated without difficulty and Zoran would only have to recreate a new, younger pack that would obey him at the beck and call.

Vasile gets angry and shakes off my grip with a sharp move. He starts pacing and making noise. Too much noise.

— So, what? We stay here, hiding like frightened rabbits, waiting for Zoran to send us back Dumitru in pieces? Mind you, you'd actually become the new Alpha. Maybe that's what you really want.

I roll up my chops and show him the fangs.

— Don't insult me. We have no chance of surviving if we attack now and if you took the time to think it over, you'd know that.

He stares at me for a moment and finally gives in with a sigh.

— OK, OK. I'm sorry. I'm sorry. I know you don't seize opportunities. What shall we do now?

— Let us follow Anton.

— Your vampire?

— Yes. It looks like he's been given orders quite different from the others, and I want to know why.

— Okay.

— Ivan, you go back to the pack territory and tell everyone to keep quiet. I don't want any individual actions.

The young werewolf accepts and turns away without waiting. He looks very happy to return to our territory, while we go after my vampire buddy. I noticed that he had fed early, which is really unusual. And who is this vampire that I've never met and who seems to discover everything from the outside world? He can't stop sniffing the air like a dog! In the beginning I thought he had spotted our spinning; but luckily, it is impossible as we are in the opposite direction of the wind. Moreover, the relationship between Anton and this vampire seems... particular. One time they ignore each other, other time they get closer. I even saw Anton holding his hand.

— Is your vampire gay?

I'm shaking my head. No. I've seen him with women before. Humans who have served him for both sex and blood. His preference has never been men. In fact, I've never even heard of homosexual vampires. I've never seen Anton get that close to one of his own either. I'd even swear that the second vampire cried at one point. Obviously, this never happened. Vampires are so famous of being bloodthirsty and heartless. They don't feel sadness, which is more of a human emotion.

— He's coming to feed off your vampire.

I don't think he's in this village to eat. He is already hiding his eyes, which will prevent him from hypnotizing his potential victims. Besides, the sunrise is close. He won't have time to get home before the first rays appear. No matter how fast he is, it's impossible. We're too far away. In fact, I see him entering a hotel.

— What's he doing?

— Let's kill him at noon. He won't stand a chance.

— No. Let's wait a little longer. He's not here just by chance. I want to know his intentions. Besides, we don't know how powerful is the vampire who accompanies him. Did you recognize him?

— It's impossible to distinguish his face with the glasses and the hood. But his gait was strange.

— Yes, you are totally right. It was... slow, for a vampire. Anton kept pace with him.

— Maybe he hasn't drunk blood for a long time.

— Um. Maybe. Let's find a spot for the night. We'll figure it out by nightfall.

— Okay. It's up to you to watch.

Although sleeping for several hours, we failed to untie all knots related to last events. In a nutshell, Zoran knows our desire for rebellion, he captured Dumitru and gathered several vampires in the castle so as to kill any fool who would venture to enter. And Anton... Anton is the biggest riddle in history, when you think of the sharp teeth. There he is coming alone towards us. I elbow Vasile's ribs to wake him up. We have to move before the vampire senses our presence

— Ah. Now the real work begins.

— No. I want to see what he's going to do.

My friend mutters in his beard.

— Why did you take me with you if we're just going to observe, without acting? You could have done it alone!

— I brought you along so you could watch my back if anything went wrong. And now shut up.

I don't understand what my partner is looking for. I don't smell any humans nearby. Besides, Anton tends to look towards trees. Really, I find his behavior confusing. Suddenly, he rushes from tree to tree with impressive agility and grabs a bird that has had the misfortune to land in its nest.

— Since when are vampires friends with fowl?

I've never seen it before. Especially when I see Anton slitting the throat of the woodcock with a sharp fingernail, holding it hanging in the air by his paws. I then notice that the animal's blood flows into a container placed on the ground.

— All right. Now I'm getting curious. Does he feed on animal blood?

— No. Only human blood.

However, Anton repeats the same action twice more until the glass is filled to the brim. He then hands the glass to the second vampire who has just appeared, a bag on his back and a whiff of shampoo in his sawing, but always with his face in the shadows.

— Here you go. Everything's fresh for the moment.

The vampire takes the container and drinks it all without leaving a drop before he takes the glass back.

— You still won't talk to me.

The silence that follows speaks for itself. Certainly, the relationship between these two is very complex. Next to me, Vasile who is as perplexed as I am and for once, wisely patient.

— Tat, look at me.

The stranger raises his head slightly. I see only a piece of skin slightly pink and nothing more. I especially notice the difference in size that hadn't struck me the day before. Anton easily looks one head taller than his fellow man. Once again, I am surprised by Anton who puts his lips on that of the second one.

— I am willing to do anything for you, even protect you from yourself. Now we have to go. We still have a long journey to get you to safety.

Anton takes his companion's hand firmly and resumes his journey, dragging the unknown vampire along strongly. We let them get a bit ahead of us so we can talk without being overheard.

— Am I the only one who thinks this vampire is the key?

I share the same point with Vasile.

— No, but the key to what?

— That's the whole point.

— Did you notice how pale Anton looked?

— Yes. He hasn't eaten.

It even slows down little by little as the night stretches on.

— He is getting weaker. This would be the perfect time to capture him and force him to tell us about Zoran's plan. It can be a means of pressure.

Vasile is wrong. Zoran doesn't care about anybody. I don't think Anton is an exception. However, he can indeed serve as an informant. The only thing that worries me is how the second vampire will react. I think we should attack him.

— Let us both jump on the stranger.

— We'll be vulnerable to Anton. We could go one-on-one. Each one his own.

I'm shaking my head.

— No. Anton cares about the other vampire for a reason we don't understand. If we can control the stranger, we can force Anton to surrender using him.

My friend is taking some time to think about it.

— That's a good idea. I'll take the left and you take the right.

— We attack at the same time, in our animal form.

— That's great. Take a break. We don't want to get Anton's attention by making noise with our makeover.

We stop and wait until they are out of sight to begin our transformation. Becoming a werewolf is not without pain. Skin and bones stretch throughout our bodies to adapt to the impressive size of the lycanthropes. Then, we cover ourselves with fur. In this form, our sense of smell is even more developed and we have no difficulty in catching up and then overtaking the two vampires.

Chapter 8

Tatjana

I am really upset. I've been in a bad situation as I didn't sleep well. I passed the entire night watching monsters and vampires fighting each other in my dreams; and in the middle of it all, Anton was pointing at me making fun of my naivety towards the world. Well, that's when I managed to get some sleep, because sleeping with a man whose desire was sinking into my lower back was not easy. Especially since I had never spent the night with anyone before and I didn't see my first night with a man going this way. I also never imagined that this man would be Anton. It only made my anger worse. In order to reveal to me that he still liked me and that he knew things about me that I didn't know. We had to be far away from the castle. Just like when we arrived in the bedroom, I took refuge in the bathroom as soon as I was awakened. Knock, knock, knock.

— I'll try to find you something to eat. Meet me at the edge of the forest and please don't let the locals see you. There are still many in the streets at the moment.

I don't even bother myself to answer him. If I open my mouth, it will only bring about insulting and threatening him, followed by begging him. Then, I will end up being even more angry at him than I am now because I am sure he has no intention of answering my questions, so I might as well keep quiet and save my breath. He must have figured it out this as he leaves the room slamming the door behind.

Once I'm alone, I take the time to look at myself in the mirror of the bathroom. The fact that we don't have a reflection is a pure myth. This morning, I think it's a shame. It would have spared me from seeing my face far too pale and my eyes brighter, more inflamed than ever with anger. I take a deep breath to relax my tense face, then I quickly run into the shower to remove the smell of Anton sticking to my skin after spending the night with his head in my neck. I thoroughly rub myself with the products that I had thought of slipping into my bag and whose lilac perfume comforts me. I've always hated living in the castle, but strangely enough, there was something reassuring about it too. I thought I would take this feeling with me thanks to

Anton and he threw it all on the floor. I'd be tempted to run away if hunger didn't twist my guts so much. I am literally starving and since I only feed on animal blood, which is less nourishing for my body than that of human, I really can't afford to go without food for even one day, unlike my bodyguard. So, I join him willy-nilly at the edge of the forest as he ordered me.

Anton hands me a glass of warm blood as soon as I get close to him.

— Here you go. Fresh off the presses.

I drink the liquid greedily, like the hungry vampire that I am, and I don't leave a drop. What's the point? Anyway, Anton won't drink it.

— You still won't talk to me.

I don't think so. I still don't feel like it, even though I am aware of the very childish behavior of my reaction.

— Tat, look at me.

I hate that nickname. That is the only thing I am sure of: I am a female vampire, the only one, if I have not been lied to on this point as well. It's unbearable to me if I pretend the opposite, even for the good cause. So, I raise my head reluctantly and in a mood. Moreover, Anton is standing overhang me with a head! I have to wring my neck towards his eyes. Or rather, his glasses. Once again, he surprises me by bending over and kissing me, gently placing his lips on mine. He doesn't wait for me to kiss him back before he withdraws, which is for the best, because I didn't react, and it's not his justification that's going to give me back my voice.

— I'll do anything for you, even protect you from yourself. Now we have to go. We still have a long way to go to get you to safety.

Anton takes my hand firmly and we resume our journey. Well, let's just say that Anton is dragging me behind him like a cannonball, because I am too shocked; and I can't put one foot in front of the other properly. My friend kissed me and swore to protect me. To protect me from myself. What does he imagine? Does that mean I may commit suicide? Or that I would do it if I learned all the nasty secrets that are hidden from me? Lost in my thoughts, I don't feel danger sneaking up on me.

Unlike Anton, who reacted only a second too late, I didn't realize the presence of these two wild beasts until I found myself between their claws. And what claws! They are impressive, thick, but tapered. They compress my throat and chest. I would be offended if someone touched my breast, but I am sure that the beast is aiming at the heart underneath. And yes, we're dead, but getting one's heart ripped out is not a pleasure. Especially since mine is still beating. Weakly, but it's beating. Although, even faintly is a bit of an exaggeration right now. Stress just made it go faster.

— Tat !!! Don't move.

Is he kidding? Anton really believes that I'm suddenly going to think I'm an overpowered vampire and that I'm going to imagine beating the two colossus that are holding me tight against them?

— What do you want Adrian? You're angry because I decided to do without your service?

Adrian ? So, one of these things has a name? I can't tell what they look like since my hood is blocking my peripheral vision. But clearly, what's gripping my windpipe is not a hand.

— We're not that close, Anton. You make your choices and I make mine. They turn out that they are now simply opposed.

The creature's voice is clearly delineated, but rumbling, biting and very rocky.

— What do you want, then?

Anton doesn't take his eyes off me as he moves with calculated slowness.

— First and foremost, I want you to stand still where you are or I'll kill your friend that you seem to care a lot about.

Anton stops instantly.

— Tat has nothing to do with our stories. Just let him go.

— I'd love to, but I want answers, and you won't give them to me unless I twist your arm.

I can see my bodyguard's pallor. He hasn't eaten since last night. He's in no condition to fight against what I suppose are two werewolves in their prime force. Besides, we've been walking for a long time. I don't know what time it is, but I'm sure time is against us, we're running out of it. I stare at Anton and nod my head imperceptibly to grant their request, as far as the iron fist on my throat allows. Anton shows me the fangs before sighing deeply.

— What do you want to know?

A spark is reflected on Anton's glasses, probably due to the predatory smile of my attackers.

— Oh ! I'm really disappointed. I wouldn't think it would be that easy.

— Release Tat and come straight to my fangs for your answers.

I've never seen Anton so... vampire. His canines are fully descended, his nails have grown into long needles and his veins are sticking out in his thin skin.

— I'm sorry, but no. I'm not crazy, and I'm less stupid, contrary to what Zoran thinks.

I see. This has less to do with me and Anton than it does with Zoran.

— Then go ahead, let's finish this!

— Hmm. You seem nervous.

My friend bends and unfolds his hands compulsively.

— Come on, let's get started before the sun comes up and you fry on the spot without saying a word. First question: where is Dumitru?

Anton shakes his head from left to right.

— You already have the answer to that question or you wouldn't be here.

— That's right, but I want you to confirm it. Besides, we have to start somewhere.

— He's in Zoran's hands.

— He's still alive?

— I don't know. I have no idea.

Even if he is, he must be in pretty bad shape. Adrian pauses, no doubt to assess the veracity of this statement.

— Okay. We'll come back to that later. How do you get into the castle without dying in the second?

— You can't. Zoran will know you're here.

— How? How does he find lycanthropes anywhere?

Anton keeps looking at me and I suddenly have the feeling that he gives them the answer without opening his mouth. That he's giving it to me, anyway. Somehow, I feel like I had something to do with it.

— Answer me.

A claw digs into the side of my neck, piercing the skin and making my blood flow.

— NO !

— He knows where the vampires are by blood ties, but we don't have a blood connection with Zoran, we know that. So, how does he do it?

I have confirmation that I had something to do with it when Anton refuses to answer once again despite my blood starting to flow more and more. Whether he answers or not, I am dead in any case. I'm screwed, so no matter how much I blame him, I don't hold a grudge to the point of dragging Anton with me into death. He can tell the moment I open my mouth, and our voices become intertwined.

— SHUT UP.

— GET OUT.

At least the grip on my throat is loosening in surprise.

— A woman???

Well, I hadn't heard the voice of my second attacker, who had been a spectator until now.

— Anton, run away.

— Zoran will do anything to get you back.

Why did my friend say that before he ran away at an alarming speed?

The two werewolves don't even try to catch him. They prefer to focus their attention on me and take off my hood with a dry gesture, freeing my hair, which starts to fall over my shoulders.

— Damn it. A female vampire!

Yes, surprise ! Looks like they'll never get over it. I can feel them looking at me like two laser beams, as if watching me for hours would change the fact that I am a woman. I'd let them continue like this for a while, but as the first light of dawn begins to appear on the horizon, I'd like these two to get over their emotions quickly.

— You've never seen women before today? Because I've never seen lycanthropes and I don't make a big deal out of it!

Okay. That's not entirely true. Now that they're holding me a little looser, I'm taking the opportunity to swivel slightly. They're really impressive. And immense! They're at least two meters high. And their muscles! They have them everywhere, protruding, mainly on their thighs.

— Don't provoke us too much, vampire, or we'll

also be the last guys you see.

— No offense, but if you don't make up your mind to move, you will.

I raise my finger in front of me to point to the beautiful orange colors on the horizon.

— She's right. We need to get her some-where safe.

— What for? Let us let her fry on the spot. That makes minus one vampire in Zoran's army.

One wants me dead, while the other one is against this idea. So, who is going to win?

— Think about it, Vasile. Anton said Zoran will do anything to get her back. We just found a way to free Dumitru.

Anton… A clever boy. Now that I think about it. I think that's exactly why he threw that sentence at me. He gave me a reprieve.

— Yeah. Or we just provoked his wrath and we'll pay for it with our lives.

— We'll know soon enough. Either way, he'll know we've been in the same place as her, so whatever we do...

Whatever they do, they're in trouble. I'd even be

happy to see my dad show up for once.

107

Chapter 9

Adrian

We have to react quickly or this vampire is going to go up in smoke in a few minutes.

— Vasile, go scout around. Find us a safe obscure shelter where we can hide and spend the day.

— We're not far from the village anymore. I can smell the humans from here.

I weigh the pros and cons in a few seconds. No, that's a bad idea.

— That's where Anton will be looking for us by sunset. This is certainly where he has found refuge for the day. It's better to keep a low profile until you come up with a plan.

— Okay.

My friend starts to trot away as if he's off on a mushroom picking trip.

— Can you please step on it? We don't have all day!

Vasile shoots me with his shiny eyes while giving

me a break before he decides to really get down to it. He drops down on all fours and goes off like an arrow.

For both of us, vampires. I really didn't expect to come across this surprise!

— Sit down, vampire.

She's not struggling with my grip on her throat, but she's not short of an answer.

— I have a first name, werewolf!

I smile in spite of myself while her long brown curls tickle my snout. Her lilac scent fills my nostrils and I realize that I love it. A little too much even. My animal part wants to rub against her and feast on her scent until it's thirsty. What does that mean? I haven't even looked her in the eyes! There's no way she's hypnotized me. Anyway, it doesn't work on my people. I scold more than I talk.

— What do you want me to call you?

— Tatjana. And you're Adrian, as I understand it.

— That's right. And now sit down.

She doesn't seem very cooperative. She's just standing there, not moving.

— If you don't let go of my throat, I'm not going to obey!

Indeed, my claws always touch her skin, ready to pierce it at the slightest movement.

— I am sorry.

I'm having a hell of a time loosening my knuckles. Not because I'm afraid she'll escape, but because I want to keep in touch with her. I fight my instincts and take a step away. She falls to the ground and I take the opportunity to finally observe her face.

She's beautiful. Her thin, slightly pinkish face is nothing austere compared to that of male vampires. She is graceful and harmoniously curved, with full lips and high cheekbones. Her eyes are always hidden by the sunglasses that eat part of her face. She looks like a human in everything. I need to remember that she's a vampire so as not to confuse the whole things. Strangely, she doesn't seem to be afraid of my lycanthropic appearance or her precarious situation. Nor does she display the arrogance that is characteristic of vampires. I'm completely baffled.

— Why are you staring at her like that? Did she hypnotize you?

I am startled when I hear Vasile's voice next to me.

— You know hypnosis doesn't work on us. I'm just curious.

He throws my clothes at my head and allows me to regain my composure.

— I found a small cave about ten yards away.

— Okay. Let's go now.

My friend lifts Tatjana up, holding her arm firmly, and I barely notice the roar that comes up in my chest. I really can't bear to see his hands on her. Damn it. There's something really wrong with me. I need a few minutes to clear my head.

— You go ahead, I'll get dressed and catch up with you.

He nods his head and pushes her in front of him, tripping her over the broken branches. My paws are hurling me to claw my packmate to the blood to let him be careful. I choose to dig my claws into my thighs instead of throwing myself at him.

I get back the human shape through struggling with my conscience. I have a little idea of the problem that assails me; and I find it so difficult to assume that. Some werewolves in the pack have already felt an attraction to a particular woman and it has always ended badly for the human, when it was not for the couple as a whole. The vampires found it very enjoyable to bite the women deliberately so that their companion would then be forced to kill them in order to prevent their transformation. Some of mine tried to defend the one that made their hearts beat, but they ended up as dead as their companion. Consequently, Dumitru demanded that we stay away from women in general. Being attracted to this female vampire is, in fact, very bad news. She could use it against me and cause my death; in case Zoran lets me live, which is not certain. I quickly check my cell phone, but nothing to worry about right now. Just a few messages from members of the pack who are getting impatient waiting for new instructions. Come on. I've already taken too long. I need to find Vasile before his fickle nature causes him to make a mistake.

It's too late for that. Vasile won't have wasted any time.

— Oh shit! What the hell just happened?

I rush to Tatjana's side. She is curled up in a corner, her naked arms are bleeding and burned badly; and the smell of charred flesh lifts my stomach.

— She tried to escape.

Well, I doubt that. No vampire is crazy enough to risk going out in the sun. Besides, the rays are just starting to break through the trees. She could have avoided them even if she couldn't have gotten far. Vasile's reckless shrug of shoulders is no more convincing than his words.

— Damn it, Vasile! We need her alive if we're going to have any leverage on Zoran.

— Then what? Where's the problem? She's alive, isn't she? After all the torture the pack was subjected to with sharp teeth, we can get a little revenge on her. She's a fucking vampire behind her angel face! Don't let her pretty face fool you. She's just a pretty gift box containing a soulless killer.

I understand his wrath. Only I see the woman side in her, not the vampire, and I can guess the pain in her pinched lips.

— If you can't stand being in the same place as her, take a walk.

— I'm not leaving you with that bloodsucker. Stop thinking with your dick. She'll bite it out of you with her teeth at any chance she gets.

I then let my beta aura surge over him to force him to obey as my cavernous voice resounds on the walls of the cave.

— Get the hell out of here!

He obeys under duress. Nevertheless, his evil gaze tells me that we won't stop at that point.

I wait until I'm sure he's far away before I pay full attention to my girl. Damn it. Sweetheart. I already think of her as my own. She is getting worse and worse, in a very fast way.

— Tatjana?

She doesn't react. She keeps her head turned to the opposite side. I put a finger under her chin and rotate her face so that it faces me.

— Tatjana? I won't hurt you.

I force myself to say:

— As long as you don't try to run away or attack me, you're safe with me.

I am pretty sure that even if that happens, I wouldn't be able to hurt her, but she doesn't need to know that.

— How are you feeling?

Her lips tremble before she decides to answer.

— It hurts. You'll be all right.

I'm not so sure about that. Her face has lost all the color and her wounds aren't healing at all. Yet the regenerative power of vampires is spectacular. Usually, their skin regains its shape within minutes, regardless of the wound. Even, we, werewolves heal just in a matter of few hours. However, in Tatjana's case, nothing happens. The burns are raw, the calcined skin is torn to shreds, and blisters form all around.

— You're not healing?

She's shaking her head.

— It takes time.

— I don't get it. Vampires heal themselves almost instantly.

She's shaking her head again.

— I don't. I am not the case.

— All right.

Maybe it's different for a female vampire. I'll think about that later.

— What can I do to help you? You need blood?

— No. No, I just want to sleep.

She's turning around again and I feel like I'm losing

her. This feeling compresses my chest and my heart. However, there is nothing I can do about it. She doesn't trust me, and rightly so, and I can't trust her despite all the things she inspires in me. I position myself at the entrance to the cave and try to rest while I wait for Zoran's inevitable call.

I only took a short nap of about two hours, on the lookout for the slightest noise, and came out of my semi-conscious state by Tatjana's groans. I approach her, but because of her dark glasses, I don't know if she is sleeping or not.

— Tatjana?

I would shake her a little to make her react, but her arms are even more damaged than before, as if the heat trapped in the burns was spreading, and I don't know where to put my hands so as not to hurt her. I decide to take off her glasses so I can see her facial expressions properly. I feel like she is asleep, but her sleep is restless. I gently caress her hair on the top of her head. It is incredibly soft, as silky as satin.

— Wake up, sweetheart.

She ends up fluttering her eyelids and I'm stuck to her eyes charm. Impossible to look away. They're just unbelievable. They're not a bottomless night sky as with all vampires, but a huge yellow-orange blaze that consumes totally my heart and soul. For the first time in my life, I feel complete.

— It hurts.

Her groaning pulls me out of my daydream.

— I'll get you a human. Feeding you will help get well.

— No. No human blood. I'm not a murderer.

Tatjana surprises me a little more every moment. I've never heard of any vampire considering himself a murderer. Instead, they think they're at the top of the food chain.

— Okay. Animal blood.

That's what Anton was giving her. I'm perfectly capable of doing the same.

— Don't leave me alone.

Her hand with the blackened fingers grabs my biceps to hold me down. Only it lacks strength. Each movement exhausts her. I realize that her skin is so pale that it becomes transparent in places, letting me guess the network of blue veins underneath. Even if I were to hunt an animal for her, there's little chance she'd be in any condition to drink when I return. It takes me no more than a microsecond to make my decision.

— Bite me.

— No. No. I've told you. No human.

— Good thing I'm not one of them. I'm a lycanthrope. Drink my blood.

— I don't want to hurt you.

— I'm safe. It's just a little bite of nothing.

I wouldn't die anyway. As for the rest... I've heard rumors about the paralysis and excruciating pain vampire venom causes us, but I've never experienced it myself. I just hope the rumors are exaggerated. However, I am willing to make this sacrifice for her and with fresh blood in her veins, she will be able to defend herself against Vasile if something goes wrong. I just hope she has enough restraint so that I don't bleed to death. I place one of my arms behind her back and the other under her thighs to position her on top of me. She has her mouth at the same height as my neck.

— I'm ready. Bite me. Do it.

She looks at me for one more moment before she pushes her impressive canines down into her jaw.

She touches them with the tip of her tongue, as if she wasn't used to pulling them out. Note, if Anton brings her blood in a glass every day, that's probably the case. She then strokes my cheek with a withered hand before plunging her teeth into my jugular.

Chapter 10

Tatjana

His beautiful yellow eyes are fearless. Yet I simply could kill him with my bite. He does trust me. It warms my heart and makes it beat a little stronger as my head spins in pain. If Adrian seems nice, his friend Vasile can't even stand seeing me, he carries a great hatred in his heart. This cruel creature pushed me into a ray of sunshine and held me there after he had taken off my coat. My arms were burnt by UV rays. What for? What mistake did I commit? I hadn't done anything to deserve this. Just being a vampire condemned me to be badly punished. I understand their resentment towards Zoran, because my father acts exactly the same way or worse. But I'm nothing like him. It's an illusion to think that being so arbitrary is better than being a vampire. Adrian's compassion touched me. I don't know why, but he really seems to care about me and sees me as a person and not as an enemy to be killed. I caress his unshaven cheek with a painful hand, taking advantage of the warmth of his body pressing against mine. I found

120

him impressive in the form of a werewolf, but his human form has nothing to envy him. I feel as if I were tiny in his arms, a fragile little flower with sharp teeth. My canines are sharper than I remember. A real sting that pierces the soft skin of his neck like a knife in butter. The first drop of blood that touches my tongue is a real electroshock. The liquid flows down my throat and spreads through my body at a cataclysmic rate, reforming my skin faster than it takes to blink. I've only swallowed a few sips and I already have no trace of burns. Plus, I've never felt so powerful, so complete, so normal. I stop sucking immediately. I have never felt a feeding frenzy and have no trouble retracting my teeth. Adrian disagrees. He leans on my skull, sticking my face to his neck.

— Keep going.

I find it so easy to get out of his grip and step back a little to look at him

— It's not necessary. I'm fit as a fiddle. I don't want to take any more blood from you than I need, otherwise you'll be weakened.

Then he opens his eyes and I'm sure I look like a complete idiot with my mouth open and my arms dangling. His eyes. His eyes have changed. They're not an exact replica of mine, however, the similarity is amazing. They have the same flame colors but keep the strange, slightly oval shape of wolves, and the iris is completely bright yellow, as when it is in the form of a werewolf.

— Are you all right? I didn't hurt you?

Adrian blinks several times and looks all around us. He's disoriented and I'm afraid I've taken too much.

— No, no, it's okay. It's just, um...

— What? Do you need anything? Do you want me to call Vasile? I knew you shouldn't have. I never drink on anyone's veins.

— Don't worry, I'm fine and it's best to leave Vasile out of it. It's just that my eyesight is... different?

— What do you mean?

— It's better.

Adrian blinks several times.

— I can see you perfectly well. Just like daylight.

If that's the whole story, then there's really no problem. I mean, um... I guess. I just hope he doesn't mind me having my eyes changed and it'll be temporary.

His hand slides under my hair and lands softly on the back of my neck.

— Feeling better?

— Yeah! Thank you.

I reach out my arms in front of me so he can see them.

— I'm totally recovered.

He slides his index finger from my palm to my shoulder, first on my right arm, then on my left, and my skin stings with goosebumps.

— You're amazing, Tatjana.

— Just a design error by Zoran.

— No. Just unique. Because you're the only female vampire, right?

I tensed up and fell off his knees at a speed that I never know I am capable of.

— Now that I've recovered, shall we move on to the interrogation?

— No !

Adrian's frowning, and I strongly feel sorry for his sad face.

— I just want to get to know you. You are not an ordinary vampire, Tatjana.

That's right. And his question is a legitimate one.

He saved my life. I owe him my cooperation. Provided that it's mutual.

— I'm the only female of my species. What about lycanthropes? Are there females?

I bite my tongue and feel a sting of jealousy squeezing my heart. I don't appreciate the image of Adrian in someone else's arms. Adrian stares at me for a moment before responding.

— No. Only men. Zoran has never created a female werewolf. At least as far as I know. I suppose the last thing Zoran wants is for our pack to be able to reproduce. Have you ever heard about it?

I'm laughing with a joyless and a giddy laugh.

— I've never heard of anything. Zoran has kept me away from the world, whatever it is, since I was born.

— Your birth? You mean, your mutation, right?

— It's all the same. I don't remember my life before.

Adrian's confused. A vein pulsates in his forehead as a result of concentration.

— I thought vampires remember their past lives just like lycanthropes?

I shrug my shoulders with feigned indifference.

— I don't. You said it yourself: I'm unique. Unique and amnesic a priori.

My interlocutor then moves closer to me and puts the back of his hand on my cheek.

— You're an exceptional vampire. Things would be very different if there were more vampires like you.

I'm leaning on his palm, enjoying the touch.

— How is it different? You mean our species isn't about to declare war on each other?

He sighs and backs off. Then the coldness of the cave hits me and I thirst for his masculine warmth.

— The situation is complicated. Zoran...

— Is my father, and I know those flaws. He will kill you to the last man for taking me away.

His eyes are glowing.

— Your dad? And you'll watch him happily exterminate us?

I let myself slide to the ground, tired of an inextricable situation.

— No. Well, for your friend Vasile, maybe. But not for you. Nevertheless, if he doesn't kill you, you'll kill him. In any case. There will be deaths. I just wish I weren't in the middle when that happens.

— You could talk to him. Convince him to release the pack.

The hope that blazes in his eyes is incredible. I'm sorry to nip it in the bud.

— I've already tried that. I've already tried to make Zoran hear that you are living beings like us. It's in vain. He wouldn't listen.

And I paid dearly for my audacity.

— You didn't know me at that time. Today you have an extra motivation and you'd probably be more convincing.

— Probably. And my punishment for going against his ideas will be similar to my vehemence. The last time he beat me and deprived me of food for three days.

— I don't get it. You're his daughter. Aren't you?

— He obviously doesn't think much more of you than he does of me. Princess is just a pompous title that means nothing when you live cooped up in a castle for two hundred years.

I'm tired of this fruitless exchange. Our peoples are more alike than they seem to think, and there is nothing I can do to save them, even if I wanted to.

For sure, I deeply want to. I want to save this beautiful wolf with extraordinary eyes who makes me feel things I've never felt before. I want to save these people who have done nothing but serve the Vampire King and his henchmen at the risk of their lives. Only the truth is, I don't have the power to do that.

— Tatjana ?

— What ?

I'm aggressive, I'm hot, and I'm fed up of everyone wanting to use me.

— We'll figure it out.

Then I doubt it. He realizes it.

— I'll find a way to free my pack and my Alpha, and I'll make sure you don't have to go back to the castle.

He sneaks up on me.

—That's what you want, isn't it? To be free, too.

— Yes. It's no more than a deceptive dream. I'm unable to manage by myself, alone. I don't have the same capabilities as other vampires. I've always had Anton by my side and I wouldn't have survived this long without his help.

He grunts when I say my friend's name and jams my face in the vise of his large hands.

— You could stay with me.

— Your people will never accept me. They hate vampires. You saw Vasile's reaction.

— I could make them do it.

— Why would you do this for me?

He puts his lips on mine. It's just a light touch, but it makes me hot, butterflies flying in my belly. I feel like I'm alive.

— Because I want to. I want to be near you. I feel a connection with you and I want to explore it.

He kisses me again, always in a very respectful way. It really makes me feel I want more. My heart is pounding. It's never been faster. I can feel it in my forehead.

— What the hell is...

Lost in the voluptuousness of the moment, I don't understand why he stopped.

— What's making that noise?

I caress the thin, short hair on his neck, scraping his skin with my thumbnail.

— What noise?

— Shh.. listen to this "bouboum, bouboum" sound.

He's patting my collarbone in rhythm with my own heart.

— It's all right. I just have a little bit of a heartbeat.

— All right, then.

Adrian grabs my lips again before he stops in the middle of our kiss.

— Hold on. Wait. What?

— Hmm?

I don't even know what we're talking about anymore. I just don't want him to stop. Anton's kisses never made me feel a tenth of the excitement I feel now.

— Is your heart beating?

— Yes. Very slowly usually, but you're over-whelming my senses.

He licks the base of my throat before coming up to my mouth and sweeping his tongue out of mine.

— My pack will accept you; I can assure you. Because you're alive.

Oh yeah, indeed alive with the body on fire. My clothes irritate my skin. I only want to take off my jeans and my tank top and rub it on Adrian. If only he could be naked, too, that would be perfect. Miraculously, he seems to hear my plea and runs his shirt over his head before throwing it to the side and doing the same with my top.

— No bra?

I sway my head from left to right, unable to align two words. Especially when Adrian grabs my nipple with his teeth, having fun hardening the tip.

— Your taste drives me crazy and your lilac smell makes my blood boil.

That makes two of us. I feel like my veins are too narrow to hold the blood flowing through them. My lover unties my belt and pulls my pants down with determination. I do the same with his pants too. His erection appears, long, hard, ready to give me an unbelievable and wonderful moment of pleasure.

Chapter 11

Adrian

This woman is going to drive me crazy. I don't know what happened when she bit me, but all my senses are heightened tenfold. I can guess the grain of her skin with every naked inch. I feel as if I'm in a field full of lilacs in bloom, with the background of her excitement's aroma. This gradually makes me drool, and my fingers itch to touch her softness. Then, I move to her second breast when the first one proudly points upwards. Meanwhile, she is scratching my scalp as she tangles and untangles my hair. I want her to mark me the way I dream of doing. My fangs are suffering because of the strong desire to get out. Our diet is much more traditional than the legends tell. Certainly, we are not cannibals, we prefer raw game. But still animal. Yet I dream of biting her and tasting her blood on my tongue exactly as she did with me. I really would like to mark her so that everyone knows she's mine, especially Anton. But unfortunately, we heal too quickly. Remembering the vampire kissing her is a torment only relieved by my sweetheart's passionate

131

response. She runs her thin fingers across my abs, drawing every hollow and bump meticulously, before wrapping her hand around my manhood. Her back and forth movements, with just the right amount of pressure, make my sap rise, and I clench my teeth so as not to come immediately. I also set to work, caressing and titillating her flesh bud, swallowing each of her groans at the source. I don't know how it came to this, but I find myself lying on the hard ground, Tatjana overhanging me and guiding me into her intimacy. Her moist heat greedily sucks me in and I grunt with pleasure when she hasn't even started to move yet.

— You're so tight.

I'm in a tight sheath that rubs on all my nerve endings with every movement. I caress her breasts that sway to the rhythm of her pelvis, playing an enticing dance. However, this is not enough. I want more. More contact, more strength. I straighten up to grab her mouth and squeeze my hands on her waist to accompany her back and forth, speeding up the pace.

— It feels so good!

Her canines glow in the dark, totally out, as well as her fangs. My face is even a little elongated, oscillating between that of a werewolf and that of a man. At the climax of the pleasure, the lycanthrope in me wins the victory and howls to death as it pours itself into the receptacle of my baby, who follows me in my pleasure by sticking her fangs into my neck. My instinct tells me to do the same and we end up exchanging fluids, both intimate and blood.

— You're mine. Never again will Anton lay hands on you or I'd kill him without a shred of pity and fry his body in the sun.

She plunges her beautiful eyes into mine and, instead of being offended by my possessi-veness, she passionately kisses me, making me taste my own blood on her lips. I have had sex before, but never so intense alike.

Tatjana has just captured me between her canines and I pray to heaven that this does not lead to my loss, or both of us.

— It's late already. We must get dressed and get some sleep before it gets dark.

Her sad look is heartbreaking.

— Then what? What's going to happen now? You'll take your way and I'll take mine? And we'll watch our people kill each other?

I finish putting on my shoes and go give her a hug.

— That's not what I want, Tatjana. I care about you very much.

I really mean it. I care about her very much. Wolves have only one female in their lives, and it seems the same for werewolves too.

— But the situation is complicated.

— I know. You have a duty to your Alpha. Anton explained to me that you've all sworn allegiance to him.

— I am part of a pack and Dumitru is its leader, just as your people obey Zoran.

I feel her arms tightening around me.

— We could run away from here. With your pack, if that's what you want.

I sigh deeply as I close my eyelids. If only it were that simple…

— I can't, Tatjana. We don't know how, but Zoran knows the position of every wolf, and he certainly knows yours because of your bloodline

— Then we have no future.

I let her reluctantly detach herself from me and lie down opposite her. As she turns her back on me, I cannot tell if she is falling asleep, but I cannot close my eyes and I always have my eyes wide open when the last rays of the sun go out on the horizon.

My cell phone rings in the first hour of the night.

— You have something that belongs to me. I want it back, and you're going to give it to me without question.

Zoran's tone makes my hair stand on end. Tatjana is mine! I decide to play the innocent, at the risk of irritating him even more.

— I don't have Anton. I don't even know where he is.

— Don't get smart with me. I got a little something you care about, too.

A scream comes into the handset and hits my sensitive ears

— You wouldn't want him to suffer because of you, would you?

His condescending tone and staging are villainous, worthy of the vampire king. I decide to go ahead with the original plan without further thought.

— Let's make an exchange.

— What for? I know exactly where you are. All I have to do is pick up my daughter and kill you incidentally.

— So, in this case, I can perfectly execute her instantly. She's much weaker than you.

Now Zoran is angry. His icy voice freezes the blood in my veins.

— How do you want to do it, werewolf?

— I want you to send Dumitru back by helicopter.

— These human machines don't work on me.

— That's the point. Get a human to lead him to me. When he gets there, Anton can come and get Tatjana. You have until sunrise.

The silence stretches between us, making me afraid I've gone too far.

— So be it. We'll do it your way.

It was a piece of cake.

— One more thing: If vampires are heading our way or werewolves don't show up, she dies. Gather your troops at the castle as you have already begun and don't let anyone move.

Zoran hangs up without answering, but his whistle of discontent speaks for itself. Then I see Tatjana staring at me.

— Your rhetoric didn't last long with Zoran.

— Sweetheart...

— It's no use. Vasile is back. I'll stay in his custody until Anton arrives. At least he was honest with me.

I have a glowing spear for a heart. What the hell did I do? I betrayed my companion without hesitation. Remorse crushes my heart, only it's too late to back down. I was afraid she would use my affection to achieve her ends. Eventually, it was me who betrayed her. Vasile is heading straight for me, and I am clearly not in the mood for the bitter remarks he will certainly make. I raise my hand to shut him up before he even opens his mouth.

— Not right now.

He quivers his nostrils and curls up his chops, showing half extended fangs.

— You smell like a vampire. And what's wrong with your eyes? What the hell did you do, Adrian?

I drop heavily to the ground and take my head in my hands.

— What did I do? Some bullshit.

The biggest bullshit of my life. The one that's going to weigh on my conscience and haunt me till the day I die.

— Fuck ! You let her trick you. You fell for her

looks and we're all going to pay for it.

— Shut up, Vasile. Tatjana is not to blame. I'm the one who fucked up. I sold her against Dumitru.

He claps with both hands like a kid. I don't know what to be happy about.

— You did it! We get our Alpha back and we get rid of the vampire. That's great news.

— How is that good news? We challenged Zoran! He caved, but he's going to make us pay! The pack is in more danger than ever and I sacrificed my mate for this!

— You followed the plan. You've...

He suddenly turns to me when he realizes what I've just confessed.

— Your girlfriend?

I nod and a stabbing pain rises up in my chest.

— Tatjana is special. I'm not even sure she's really a vampire. Her heart is beating, Vasile. She doesn't drink human blood. She doesn't heal at high speed.

— Her arms look okay, though.

I don't want to go into details, so I'm vague.

— I treated her.

My friend jumps on top of me, straddling me to get the collar off my shirt, and I can't stop him. The two holes marking the entrance of her canines are still visible in the hollow of my neck.

— She bit you! She looks like a vampire!

I unsettle him and Vasile spreads out beside me in a growl.

— I wouldn't have had to if you hadn't hurt her and she only took what she needed. Just a few sips. And I didn't have any side effects.

— No paralysis?

I shake my head negatively.

— No pain?

— No. Not a thing.

— Well, there's your eyes. They look different.

— I can see better than before. I can hear further too and my sense of smell is better.

— You mean instead of hurting you, her venom made you better?

— Looks like it, yeah.

— This is... unexpected.

I'm sure it is. And how do I thank her for the gift

that she gave me unintentionally? By sending her back to the castle, where she's even less free than the pack.

Vasile puts one hand on my shoulder and we stare at Tatjana's back, sitting further back.

— Once we're free of the Vampire King, maybe you could go get her. I'm not saying it's going to be easy to get her accepted by the pack, but if that's what you want...

Vasile has deeply touched me by his unexpected reaction.

— Thank you, Vasile. Thank you for understanding. Only how do you think she'll feel when we kill her father and her people? Do you really think she'll want to stay with the murderers of her family? If one of us doesn't kill her first.

— I'm going to spread the word to the pack. No one will touch the female vampire. She's your woman. I'm sorry I hurt her feelings badly. You're right, she's different. She didn't even try to hurt me while I was holding her under UV light. I'm going to make some calls, and you should go talk to her. I can feel her anger from here. Vampire or not, a woman holds a grudge. Don't let her get away from you like that.

My friend's right. I need to explain before it's too late. I don't want our forced separation to widen the crack between us any further. However, I don't have the opportunity. I feel Anton before I see him. Long before. He finally comes out of the thickets and shoots me out of the air, his eyes full of hatred towards me.

— You're an idiot, Adrian.

That's the second time I've heard it today. I'm going to believe it. So, he walks over to my girlfriend and sits down beside her, putting one arm on her shoulder. My wife then puts her head there and I can't stand it any longer. I prefer to go back to the cave before making an irreparable error and behead my old partner. I leave them under Vasile's watch.

<u>Chapter 12</u>

Tatjana

The feeling of betrayal burns deeply inside me exactly like burning UV rays. I feel like I'm suffocating, I'm not even able to breath, and my heart beats in a slow motion, as if it's finally dead. If only that were the case, I would suffer less from believing him when he was just playing me. He only wanted answers and I gave them to him effortlessly. I'm a lousy and naive vampire; I get fooled easily. Anton's right: Not only do I have childish behaviors, but I am a child indeed. And it is high time to grow up. It's a long past time. At two hundred years of age, it becomes a matter of survival so as to avoid being swallowed up by darkness and bitterness.

— Good evening, princess.

I didn't think I'd feel so much joy seeing Anton again. All he has to do is turn me against him so that I will completely fall apart. My tears start to run down my face and I can't, or even try to hold them back. My heart is broken and I need a friend

142

more than ever. I am entirely aware of the fact that Anton has always been there for me and has always protected me, even though he hides things from me. I know I can count on him.

— Calm down, Tatjana. I can't bear to see you so unhappy. They won't hurt you. I'll fix everything right now. I'm not leaving without you this time.

He forces me to look him in the eyes and all I see is blackness that freezes my heart.

— I promised to be beside you and protect you, and I'll keep my promise, forever. Did the boys hurt you? I don't see any wounds on you.

Anything wrong? Yes and no. My soul is much more bruised than my body and I don't want to have to explain to him how my wounds have healed so I'd rather lie to him.

— No, they didn't hurt me.

He doubtfully looks at me again for a while.

— Okay. I guess fear has gotten on your nerves. Now princess, take this and drink it up. As soon as Dumitru arrives, we'll get moving without wasting any time, and above all, without giving the werewolves any second of time to take us both prisoners.

— It's okay. I can't wait to get away from here. But, I'm not hungry, Anton.

— You need to be fully strong. You will have to run quickly. You can't afford to make it if you don't take some energy.

My stomach is so knotted that it is lifted by the first drop of blood. I'm heartily shaken.

— I'm sorry, Anton. I can't swallow anything.

He takes the glass out of my hands before the smell makes me throw up for real.

— All right. You don't have to insist. You obviously won't keep it. So, listen to me, When I give you a sign, hold on to me very tightly and don't let go.

I don't understand his instructions and I don't care.

— All right.

We sit there for a long time, half asleep, until the sound of helicopter blades is heard. My father kept his word. The helicopter lands several meters away. It couldn't get any closer, showing signs of failure because of the vampires' presence, me and Anton. This is the first time I've seen one and I'm impressed with the evolution and the ingenuity of humans. They're far from being a sub-race either.

It's quite obvious that Zoran knows no more about the modern world than I do. The human at the controls descends from the aircraft and carries on his arms a man in very bad situation. I can feel his blood from here, stinging my nostrils and making my canines tremble. I clench my jaws to prevent them from coming down. That's not the case with Anton, who salivates at the sight.

— You wait here. I'll be back in a second.

— Anton, no.

— I have orders, Princess.

I fear for a moment that he will attack Adrian, who has run to his alpha to help him walk, but he just jumps on the poor human like a cobra and plunges the canines into his flesh. I can't take it anymore and look away, the nausea coming back.

— Adrian's right. You are a unique vampire.

Vasile's voice behind my back startled me.

— I'm different, yes. I thought lycanthropes were beings who deserved my mercy. I was mistaken.

— Adrian wouldn't...

That's all I hear. Anton hits me with superhuman force, lifts me up in his arms like a straw and carries me away at breakneck speed.

— Hang on tight, princess. We will get as far as we can before sunrise.

I realize we could have made the journey much easier and faster if I had been a real vampire. Anton kept up with my pace. Now we're following his and I suspect we'll be back at the castle very soon. Eventually he stops in a small abandoned village just before the first light of dawn.

— We'll be back at the castle tomorrow.

— Good.

I can't hold back the question that burns my tongue.

— Then what now? What happens now?

— War, Princess. Zoran won't let the werewolves throw such an affront at him without a bloody response. He'll get revenge, probably wipe out the whole pack, starting with Vasile and Adrian. Dumitru is no longer a threat in his current state. The Vampire King has beaten him badly. It will take him several days to recover from the tortures he suffered. Besides, if he ever does, Zoran will surely end up with him.

No. no, no, no. I don't want Adrian to get beaten up, tortured or slaughtered. Despite his betrayal, he brought my heart back to life for a short moment. I wish him freedom and peaceful life. Even being away from me. A tear comes out of my eye again.

— I know you're against this war. Nevertheless, there's nothing you can do about it and you know that.

— What if the vampires come together to make Zoran see reason? You've spent a lot of time with the lycanthrope. Surely, you've made friends?

How could it be otherwise? I only spent one day with Adrian and I fell in love with him. How could vampires and werewolves have spent decades together without making any connection and friendships?

— You don't understand Tatjana! Zoran leads us all, vampires and lycanthropes alike. Do you think you're the only one who's suffered the wrath of the king? Please, open your eyes! The few vampires who tried to protect their werewolf pairing ended up being burned and their wolf skinned. All the supernatural beings and forces obey Zoran like robots or die by his hand. So, if I were you, I would shut up and forget about what happened in that cave.

— What?

I did not talk about anything. What does he mean by that?

— Don't think I am a fool. I got a good look at Adrian's eyes. A striking resemblance to yours. I'm just wondering what made you go against what you believe.

Attraction and trust.

— Just survival instinct.

Anton shakes his head in displeasure.

— You're still a bad liar, princess. And now you should get some sleep.

Adrian

Dumitru is really in a very bad situation. He's not dead, but he almost is. His eyes are horribly swollen. There are traces of purple and ulcerated fangs in every bit of his skin in addition to the deep scratches that crisscross his body, and some of his limbs are cut and put at a strange position of his damaged body.

— Alpha ! You have to transform.

— Can't.

His voice is only a hoarse whisper and blood flows from his mouth.

— Too much venom.

He's paralyzed with vampire venom. I am the only one who knows and experiences a venom that has a very different effect. Well, it costs almost nothing to try. Dumitru will think I'm crazy. As for my girlfriend... She already thinks I used her; that's not going to settle her opinion about me.

— Vasile, make Tatjana come.

— Impossible. I can't do it.

— Don't start that again. Bring just her for Dumitru.

— Stop yelling at me. She's already gone.

I almost let go of Dumitru from my hands.

— What?

— I'm sorry. Anton took her with him as soon as you joined our Alpha.

No ! I lost her and I didn't even have time to apologize. Only God knows when I'd see her again or even whether I'd ever see her again or not. Just thinking about her bleeds my heart

— Adrian, Dumitru needs us. Get moving. We'll think of a solution later.

Vasile is right. We don't have much time before the vampires get to us. They're just stuck for the day, but the next night will be inevitable.

— We'll put him in the cave. I've got an idea. We'll see if it works.

I slash my palm with a sharp claw and my blood starts beading through the gash.

— What are you doing?

— My companion's venom is circulating in my blood. I hope it can help Dumitru heal, even partially, so that he can transform himself.

— Hmm. We can always give it a try.

I force my Alpha to drink my blood, sticking my hand to his mouth until he soaks up enough.

— Look at me, Adrian.

Dumitru's wounds are slowly healing as he swallows. It's not as effective as if Tatjana had injected it directly into his veins, but it's enough for Dumitru to regain consciousness and a kind of clarity.

— How long did I sleep?

— You only have passed out for a few minutes.

He frowns at me.

— With all the venom in my system, I must have been thunderstruck for one week at least.

— We'll talk about it later. Turn around. You need

to get better.

His mutation is extremely exhausting. The alpha is painfully contorting on the stone floor, howling, screaming and sweating, while his limbs are hardly covered with black fur. His muscles inflate and deflate several times before taking place on a disproportionate body for now. He ends up in the body of a werewolf with a human face, scratching his skin as his nose struggles to transform into a snout. At the end of an eternity, our alpha finally has his lycanthropic form and moans, panting under suffering. Never has a metamorphosis been such an ordeal.

— You think it's Zoran's venom or the venom of...

— Shh. Shh.

I don't feel like telling Dumitru about Tatjana right now. He already had a boundless hatred with sharp teeth. His recent stay at the castle certainly did not put him in a better mood. And of course, he won't accept my companion. Vasile is right. I'll undoubtedly find a way to get her back. There is no other alternative.

— Find a way to fly that helicopter. We need to join the pack and come up with a defensive plan.

— All right. And you, transform yourself, just the

time to be fixed.

Good idea. If my metamorphosis goes smoothly, it is because my wife has nothing to do with Dumitru's problem.

My transformation has never been smoother or faster. No pain, no latency. I think I'm even heavier than before and my size has increased. I stand at the entrance of the cave to breathe in the air. I can distinguish all the smells over a very long distance. I smell all the rodents, the essence of the helicopter, the moss growing on the trees. And Vasile is running towards me.

— Whoa!

— I am different?

— Yes and no. You look like a werewolf, but you're taller and squarer than before. And your teeth...

— I don't have fangs anymore?

I pass my tongue over my fangs and sting myself on sharp teeth.

— You still have your wolf fangs, but you also have sharp fangs like a vampire's.

Definitely. This trip never ceases to surprise me. I knew that nothing would be the same after meeting my girlfriend. I could never have imagined how true that was.

Chapter 13

Tatjana

I've never seen a big number of people at the castle. There are vampires wherever I turn my eyes. They look at me in a curious, lecherous or snarling way. I get closer to Anton instinctively as he leads me to Zoran's quarters.

— Just relax. You smell fear in your face. It excites them.

— I thought Zoran wanted me to keep my existence a secret.

— Looks like things have changed. Stay close to me and whatever happens, obey Zoran.

As if I used to challenge my father. Well, this happens to me. However, in this very tense environment, I really do not want to risk it.

I feel a little less oppressed in the king's quarters, strangely empty compared to the castle's corridors. Unfortunately, this lasts only for a moment, until my gaze falls on the butcher's shop on the floor. No longer does a living soul moan or beg for mercy, for the simple reason that all humans are dead, the arms of some still attached to the wall while their bodies are no longer. No risk of transformation for them. Not a single one has his head anymore.

— Stop staring at them.

I immediately turn my head towards Anton as I hear his weak voice. I feel something bitter in my mouth and my sight is misty with tears that refuse to flow.

— Here you are at last, my daughter.

Zoran is on his throne, like a lord of ancient times. What's the difference? He is covered in blood, like a sinister reminder of the events that took place here.

— I apologize for the chaos, but my servants are undisciplined, as you both know Excuse the mess, but my servants are undisciplined, as you both know.

The chaos? These poor humans are nothing more than an inconvenience to be cleaned up? The rage fights for the place of sadness in my heart. How can life be so despised?

— Anton. Did you get rid of them?

I have a hell of a time keeping a neutral face. I know exactly who Zoran is referring to.

— I didn't get the chance. I preferred to put Tatjana's safety first. All I could do was eliminate the pilot of the helicopter.

He's lying. He could have killed Vasile and Adrian when he found me. I was sitting far away from them. He chose not to do it against the king's orders.

— You disappoint me for the second time. Be careful it's not the last, Anton.

For the first time, I realize what my friend told me: vampires don't have a better fate than werewolves. Zoran rules everyone with an iron fist.

— Come here, daughter.

I then step towards him out of obligation more than out of desire. The smell of death floats around my father like a gloomy perfume.

— My dear girl. My greatest creation.

Zoran never looked at me that way before. He seems so pleased with himself.

— Those wolves had you in their hands and they let you go.

He starts laughing out loud. A sadistic, soulless laugh, a laugh from beyond the grave. A growing uneasiness creeps into me. I take a look at Anton, who seems as uncomfortable as I am.

— They had found what they had been looking for, for decades without even knowing it, and they gave you back to me.

Why would the wolves be looking for me? They didn't even know I existed. My father grabbed my face with a firm hand and scratched me with his sharp fingernails as I passed.

— Oh, yes, you're my finest work, my masterpiece.

— I don't get it.

— Of course! You never understood anything!

His arrogance stings my feelings.

— Then explain it to me!

I quickly pull myself together before my vehemence costs me dearly. Head down, I repent at his feet

— Explain to me, Father.

He takes the time to scrutinize me carefully.

— I don't see why not. In any case, the wolves are doomed and that traitor Dumitru must be dead by now.

It pains me to know that Adrian's pack has lost its Alpha. No matter what I do, the wolf is always in my thoughts.

— I bit you two hundred years ago.

Thank you, I'm aware of that. If there's nothing more I can learn from him... I'll keep my lips sealed until I hear something new.

— I was going to make you my meal, but you surprised me. It hadn't happened since I was brought back to life in that dung pit.

He's got his eyes in the air, remembering the moment my life turned upside down.

— What have I done to surprise you?

His dark eyes plunge into mine.

— When I was about to suck your blood to feed myself, you said you forgave me. Instead of struggling and begging me to let you live like everyone else do, you told me you forgave me, that everyone had to feed themselves.

I'm glad to hear that human or vampire, I've always had an open mind.

— You were part of high society, but you weren't

arrogant like the other nobles. You'd rather help the common people than strut your stuff in luxury. I let you live that day.

Is that what he thinks? He still turned me into a vampire!

— I know what you're thinking. Nevertheless, I didn't turn you into a vampire that night. I didn't really turn you into a vampire. You're different.

I already knew that. What I'd like to know is why?

— What made me different?

— I didn't drain you of your blood until your heart stopped beating. When it started to slow down sharply, I made you drink my own blood to heal you.

— Then what am I?

— Half vampire. Half human, half vampire. You're more alive than dead.

— Why can't I remember?

— Because I've decided so, of course. You are the queen of the werewolves after all!

I'm choking to death at the same time as Anton, who's hiccoughing behind my back. Like, he didn't know everything.

— Hey ! What are you thinking about? Ah, do you think that I showed mercy? Oh, come on. Don't insult me! I mostly thought you were the weakling being I was looking for. With your extraordinary blood, I've given life to my army of werewolves. With your compa-ssionate side, I figured they'd be as malleable as you are. In fact, I turned your two brothers first. It turned out Andrej and Dumitru were far less docile than you.

— Dumitru?

— And yes. The Alpha himself. I was sure that this way, even if he found you, he'd never kill you and he had no reason to look for you since he thought you were dead. It's a pity Andrej accidentally came into your room. I had to kill him to shut him up and that turned Dumitru against me.

The man in my room. The one Zoran killed in front of me without my knowing who he was. A tear beads in the corner of my eye for my brothers who died because of me.

— Don't be sad. They're just dogs, born on the full moon thanks to your defective blood and a cocktail of my own composition. And now you're going to help me find the others, one by one until we exterminate this vermin.

Now, I get it. The blood ties. Zoran knows where every vampire is because of the blood ties. It's my own blood that leads him to the lycanthropes.

— Never.

His hand is splitting and clutching my throat.

— Excuse me ?

— I would never help you kill my family.

Because that's what werewolves are. My family, like vampires. I'm the link between them, the bridge that could bring everyone together with a little effort. Zoran squeezes his hand and I can barely swallow.

— Zoran…

— If you want to save Anton's life, I advise you to think about your next words.

A silence stretches between us.

— All you have to do is hypnotize her to make her cooperate.

— What do you think I've been doing for the last two hundred years?

— You absolutely do. I meant no disrespect.

— Leave us alone now. If you want to make yourself useful, get the troops together. We're going to war.

— It's as good as done.

Anton's promise to protect me didn't last long; I got another stab in my already battered heart as the door closes behind him. Zoran definitely makes all relationships dirty just by opening his mouth.

— Don't look so disappointed. What were you thinking? That his love for you would surpass his devotion to his king? Oh, please! Please! Don't be so naive. Anton is a vampire. Vampires don't love anyone.

Certainly, the Vampire King doesn't love anyone, but I thought Anton was totally different.

— Now, let's get down to business. We have a race to wipe off the face of the Earth.

I close my eyes by reflex. In books, vampires hypnotize their victims by looking them in the eye. I always thought that was part of the folklore and the ritual. Now that I know it isn't, I assume the rest is true too, and I have no intention of making it easy for Zoran. If I understand correctly, without me he won't have any way of tracking down the werewolves, and I intend to protect them, even if it's the last thing I'd do.

— You think you're smart? You're just postponing

the inevitable.

His fingernails dig into the soft skin of my neck.

— I could make you bend to my will. You're nothing. Without me, you wouldn't even exist.

He soon forgot that I am his greatest creation. It's all just nothing. I'm just a tool in the hands of the vampire king and it has only lasted too long.

— I'd rather die than help you.

— Don't test me.

His sharp canines pierce the skin on my collarbone, but he abruptly removes his mouth at the first suck.

— What the hell is...

I blink to see his face shocked, then furious and mad with rage.

— What did you do? YOU HAVE DEFILED MY WORK! You have spoiled everything!

He throws me off as if I am a plastic bag and I crash among the corpses of humans. My hands slip on the sticky blood when I stand up somehow. I only have time to get down on my knees when Zoran tears the collar of my shirt.

— You allowed one of them to put their mark on you!

Yes, I was bitten by a werewolf. To say that he made his mark... I'm nobody's property. With my fingers, I touch the teeth marks that cause a bulge in my skin. Zoran takes the opportunity to stare at me and his pupils dilate before I react. Only nothing happens.

— That monster changed you!

That's for sure. Definitely, he did.

— You're no longer useful to me! Hypnosis doesn't work on wolves! And now it won't work on you either.

He punches me so hard with his right hand letting me fall on the floor with my cheekbone exploded. After that, he sends me flying across the room with a kick to the ribs, before piercing me with his hand to grab my beating heart at an unusual speed.

— You will pay for this betrayal. But first, you're going to feel and see them die in front of your eyes, all of them. You will feel every blood tie break as I rip their hearts out.

He grabs a handcuff attached to a huge chain anchored in the wall and puts it around my wrist. The metal bites my skin and makes it blister at every point of contact.

— Silver doesn't mix well with unclean blood. And

now, if you don't mind, I have a cattle hunt waiting
for me.

Chapter 14

Adrian

Our return to the pack territory was quite smooth at the end of the day and we landed just before nightfall. Dumitru still has a few wounds, but his healing is still amazing. At this moment, he is waiting for my explanations; but I am hesitant to explain what happened. I've been circling around like a wolf in a cage for several minutes, while Vasil and my alpha are watching and scrutinizing me. Suddenly, my phone rings just as I'm about to open my mouth. I thank this reprieve, until I see the caller's name on the screen. Anton. I thought we'd already told each other everything. What does he want from me? Just thinking of Tatjana in his arms crushes my heart. The ringing stops, then it starts again.

— Who's calling you insistently?

— it's Anton.

I stare at my cell phone as if it were the first time, I've seen one.

166

— Answer him. It might be about your girlfriend.

Vasile's words hit me like an uppercut and I pick up the phone so fast that I almost smash it to the ground.

— Meet me at the edge of the forest.

Too cold, too direct. My lips curl up in this dry order.

— Why is that?

— To save the princess. If I'm not mistaken, you care for her as much as I do.

Save her? Zoran is her father. He would never dare...

— Stop thinking and bring the pack. We're going to need a big number of warriors ready to fight. I'll take charge of gathering vampires who are fed up with doing Zoran's bidding.

There's no time to argue or find out more. Anton's already hung up.

— You want to explain now?

— I'll explain later. We need to regroup at the tree line.

— I think you forget I'm the alpha here, so you'd better tell me what the hell is going on. Nobody's going anywhere.

I'm growling at Dumitru, showing him the fangs.

— Go ahead, challenge me. You might win. Personally, I got plenty of time. What about you, Dumitru?

He's smart. Yes, I could win our fight. First of all, I don't want his job, and second, I have no time to lose.

— Anton's going to gather some vampires to fight Zoran with us.

— Why would he do that?

— He's in love with the only female vampire in existence and she's in Zoran's hands.

— That's interesting information, but what does this have to do with us?

— She's also my mate.

Dumitru sees red. So furious.

— You bonded with a vampire?

I'm pissed off too. I want us to leave. Now, now!

— Yes, and you should thank me. It was his venom in my blood that cured you! She's different. She's unique.

That's what shut him up, at last.

— She changed your eyes.

— She made me stronger.

Dumitru sighs deeply.

— Okay, we'll talk about it later. Let's go. But actually, we should leave a few wolves behind. Who knows? it may be a trap.

Anton is waiting for us, he is turning round in a circle, terribly nervous.

— You took too much time!

— I am not the leader of the pack.

He doesn't need to say a word any more. His eyes turn to Dumitru, who angrily stares at him in the eyes.

— You should be as excited about this attack as we are.

— I'm thrilled to attack the castle, only I don't see why I should rescue a vampire in the process.

— It's obviously pity that you feel that way. I thought Tatjana would still matter to you even though she became a vampire.

Dumitru's turning as white as snow, waxier than Anton, who clearly fed well.

— Tatjana?

— Yes, Tatjana, your sister.

— She died a long time ago.

— No. She became a princess, a prisoner for two hundred years. And now, let's go, before he decides to kill her.

I'll stop him by my strength.

— Why would he do that?

— Because you're not the only one who's changed.

He doesn't need to say any more. Like vampires, we have venom in our fangs. Usually having no effect on vampires, I didn't think for a second that with my mate everything was different.

The castle loomed in the distance, gloomy, huge shadows in the night. Everything is too quiet there. I'm able to see in the dark, better than my brothers, I can detect furtive movements to the north and south. The loyal vampires to Zoran are waiting for us with a vengeance. Anton has assured us that the Vampire King will not sense our approach, but he's prepared for that. Dumitru divides us into two groups to attack simultaneously on both flanks and takes the lead of one battalion, while I take the lead of the other one. I am closely followed by Anton, who did the same with the vampires. With those few sharp teeth on our side, we are evenly matched. So, victory is not guaranteed. We move forward in hushed steps and let the vampires pass in front of us, taking the time to transform ourselves.

— Anton. I thought you were one of those traitorous deserters.

— There are no deserters.

Anton then plunges his hand into his interlocutor's chest, tearing his heart out with one hand while tearing his throat with his fingernails of the other hand. At least I no longer have any doubt about his serious involvement in this war. So, we all throw ourselves into battle, all canines and fangs are out, playing claws and nails to be the first to slit the opponent's throat. Fingernails dig into my flesh as I slice an enemy's tendons cleanly to make him fall to the ground and bite him savagely on the neck; I break his spine carefully before tearing his windpipe. My mouth fills with blood that tastes pungent and repulsive, very different from the sweet taste of my companion. The fact of thinking about her for a while makes me distracted. As result, I don't see a vampire who rushes at me takes advantage of the situation to push his nails down my shoulder to the bone, making me scream in pain. I scratch the void to free myself from this close contact and finally reach his face, deep enough to tear his cheek to the jaw and make him let go. I am amazed to see my wound recovers at the same speed as my attacker's, but my surprise doesn't last long. Wolf howls can be heard in the distance, proof that all is not going well, and the comrades around me are not in a better position. The vampires are slowly but surely pulling us back, away from the castle, away from my destiny. The shadow of Zmei Gorynych is taking shape in the moonlight and a crazy idea crosses my mind.

— Adrian, what the hell are you doing? This is no time to be daydreaming in front of the goddamn statue!

— I... nothing.

Anton's right. The lycanthropes are being slaughtered despite the help of the anti-Zoran vampires.

— If you have any ideas, no matter how crazy, go ahead! We're losing and we won't get a second chance! Zoran will be here soon...

He doesn't have to finish his sentence. When the Vampire King comes to the battlefield, it'll all be over. He will exterminate all those who have rebelled against him, regardless of race.

I remember the legend of the thousand-year-old dragon as I head to him, protected by Anton and Vasile who are fighting fiercely. Only extraordinary blood and a princess in distress can awaken the dragon. As for the second part, we're good, as for the first one... Let's hope that a blood mixing human, lycanthrope and vampire characteristics is extraordinary enough to bring him out of his long sleep. I slash my paw with a claw and caress the colossus' leg, leaving a trace of fresh blood on the stone. I repeat the same thing several times, the wound closing quickly each time, and leave scarlet marks on the body, tail and heads of this stone giant. Meanwhile, the battle rages around me, my brothers struggle to defend themselves and some mourn the loss of their friends.

The sudden silence that rises suddenly freezes my blood. The cold comes down on me like an evil wave, and all eyes are turned to a point outside my field of vision.

— Did you really believe you could defeat me?

Zoran's devilish laughter resounds in the silence of the night and echoes over the statue of Zmei like an echo of bad omen.

— I am your creator, your master at all. You are nothing without me. The last one who forgot this truth paid dearly for it.

The sound of a body hitting the ground knots my stomach more than Anton's cry of hate.

— TATJANA!

I'm afraid to find out what's behind the three-headed dragon, but my feet lead me to it automatically. My companion is there, bleeding, with multiple wounds on her body. I run towards her and literally push Anton to take her in my arms.

— My sweetheart. What did I do? What did I do? I should have kept you close.

Zoran is getting dangerously close to my position as vampires and werewolves circle around us. Looks like it's all going to come down to him and me and the outcome of our fight will determine the outcome of this war. I can see Dumitru in the crowd, nodding his head and looking into my eyes. By this simple gesture, he gives me his trust and gives me full power. I will fight in the name of the pack.

— So, you're the sly one who defiled my daughter. I had a choice between two dogs and I didn't know which one was responsible for her death.

Dead? I press my ear to her chest and I hear with relief a "boom", weak, but there. That's all that matters. My companion is alive. Just barely, but alive. I carry her delicately to the person who will protect her as ferociously as I do: her brother, who hides his emotion poorly. Her moist eyes are a reflection of mine. I take the time to whisper one last recommendation to her before turning around, ready to face my sworn enemy.

I run out, head first and shout forward. Zoran avoids me with disconcerting ease and gives me a pat on the back.

— You're a meaningless dog. You don't even deserve that I get tired.

He throws himself in the air and falls on my shoulders, clinging to my fur and sticking his canines deep into my skull, just between my ears.

— NO !

My companion's voice pierces the fog that has invaded my mind and distracts Zoran. I ride like a wild horse and bewilder him, sending him flying away. Unlucky, he falls back on his feet as I shake my head to clear my mind. A gentle hand caresses my head and the tips of my ears.

— Adrian.

I squeeze my girlfriend's waist blindly and hug her tightly against me. Dumitru didn't hesitate to give her blood as I asked him to. He saved his sister and gave me back my love.

— My wife. I'm sorry. I will never leave you again.

— Shhh. Later on.

She lays a light kiss on my snout and an angry howl slams into the night sky.

— You're both going to die. My followers are with me.

The unthinkable happens then. The ground vibrates beneath our feet, dust flies in all directions and the dragon Zmei awakens to life. His heads straighten and his tail strikes the ground with vigor. His nostrils dilate, releasing smoke with each exhalation. His piercing eyes scan the surroundings, staring at vampires, werewolves, and the unusual couple I form with Tatjana. I pass her by reflex behind me to protect her from... everything. Zoran has stopped with his people and stares at the dragon in amazement. It's surprising, of course. Then he makes a fatal mistake. He's playing the king.

— Dragon monster, I am King Zoran and I command you to obey me. Kill the dogs and the woman who supports them.

A wall of protection is forming around me and my wife, made up of wolves as well as vampires.

A voice rises in the air, ethereal, unreal, resounding between my ears like the roll of a drum.

— The princess has chosen her king. And the people support them. Either submit or die.

Zoran rebels against this demand.

— He will not. I am their creator, I am...

He'll never finish that sentence. The dragon swells his throat, fills the glands in it, and spits out an impressive flame that burns everything in its path. The incandescent skeleton of the vampire king crumbles to a pile of ashes on the ground, followed closely by the few reckless vampires trying to defeat an opponent ten times their size.

— Lead wisely, Princess. You are the bond that unites your people.

<u>Epilogue</u>

Tatjana

Zoran's disappearance has clearly brought about a peaceful life. Everyone's living in harmony, no conflict and no fear anymore. It was a time of great changes and great decisions. Not all of them were easy to accept, neither by the werewolves nor the vampires, but all of them were necessary. Fortunately, I have the unconditional support of a trio of shockers, by my side. Anton, Dimitri and Adrian are nurturing me like a mother with her little one. Finding out I had a brother really was a wonderful surprise. Every day, he takes the time to visit me to tell me about my life before my transformation. He tells me that I am not very different from when I was born. We also mourned our brother, Andrej. Too much. This brother, who was barely seen, who died because of me. Dumitru doesn't hold it against me. But I still feel guilty about it. Anton is... still Anton. He is always by my side, even when he had to make room for Adrian. Jealousy soon gave away to acceptance, and I wouldn't get away with it with the vampires if he didn't support all of my orders. Among which the biggest one is: no more human deaths. My people understand the necessity, but the application... So, it was agreed that each vampire would only hunt in the presence of a werewolf. In this way, the vampire hypnotizes his prey so that he has no memory of the encounter and the lycanthrope forces him to let go before it's too late. Werewolves also didn't like this proposal either. Fortunately, as the vampires showed respect for their mate, tensions released. Moreover, thanks to my brother's study of my venom, the werewolves now have the same longevity as mine. Which is perfect, because I can't imagine living without Adrian.

Adrian is the source of my strength. Indeed, he is everything in my life. He is the reason for my existence. He always takes care of me. He shows me, through each of his actions, romantic words, a kiss, a gift; as well as admitting that I am the one who fulfills his life as he mesmerizes mine too. And every day, we go to stand at the foot of Zmei, as recognition of the incredible gift he has offered us: a peaceful life together among our own.

<u>Also By : Viginie T.</u>

Paranormal romance

Guardian Angels Pack Series: - Connor

- Sean

- Nate

The Ottawas Series : - My Ottawa Lynx

- My Ottawa Eagle

- My Ottawa Beaver

- My Ottawa Bear

Fallen Angels Series : - Dance my angel

- Flee my angel

- Colors of the Dragon

Facebook : Viginie T.